THE RAINBOW PEOPLE

Also by Laurence Yep

SWEETWATER

DRAGONWINGS

CHILD OF THE OWL

KIND HEARTS AND GENTLE MONSTERS

DRAGON OF THE LOST SEA

THE SERPENT'S CHILDREN

DRAGON STEEL

MOUNTAIN LIGHT

LAURENCE YEP
THE RAINBOW PEOPLE

illustrated by David Wiesner

———————— HARPER & ROW, PUBLISHERS ————————
Grand Rapids, Philadelphia, St. Louis, San Francisco, London,
Singapore, Sydney, Tokyo, Toronto
————————————— NEW YORK —————————————

Typography by Joyce Hopkins
2 3 4 5 6 7 8 9 10

Library of Congress Cataloging-in-Publication Data

people / Laurence Yep ; illustrated by David Wiesner.

A collection of twenty Chinese folk tales that were
passed on by word of mouth for generations, as told by some
old-timers newly settled in the United States.
ISBN 0-06-026760-7 : $
ISBN 0-06-026761-5 (lib. bdg.) : $
1. Tales—China. [1. Folklore—China.] I. Wiesner, David, ill.
II. Title.
PZ8.1.Y37Rai 1989   88-21203
398.2'0951—dc19   CIP
                                                          AC

To Darrell Lum,
A far better storyteller

Contents

INTRODUCTION

When my father picked fruit in the Chinese orchards near Sacramento, the workers would gather in the shack after a hot, grueling work day; one of the ways that the old-timers would pass the time before sleep came was to tell stories.

But these stories were far from escapist maneuvers. What Kenneth Burke said of proverbs is equally true of folktales: They are strategies for living. At the very least, the stories offered consolation and more often hope. But beyond that, the stories also expressed the loneliness, anger, fear, and love that were part of the Chinese-American experience.

The old-timers were among the Chinese who were unable to bring their families to America. Although they were married and had children, they lived most of their lives as bachelors. Their life-style has endured from 1848 to our own time. One can still find the old-timers down in Portsmouth Square in San Francisco.

However, there were a few Chinese who were able to bring their wives over and start families here, and by the 1930's there was a small but sizeable number of Chinese girls and boys whose entertainments and tastes were very much like those of their white contemporaries. But in most cases, these young Chinese still dwelled in a Chinatown with the old-timers. And almost all of them could have traced their roots to less than a dozen counties in Kwangtung province in China.

Previous collections consist of Chinese tales taken from the many provinces of China—especially the northern ones. Trying to understand Chinese-Americans from these tales is like trying to comprehend Mississippian ancestors by reading a collection of Vermont folktales. Some tales come from a common heritage; but others are specific to the region.

As part of a WPA project in the 1930's, Jon Lee collected tales in the Oakland Chinatown. Sixty-nine of these were translated by him and subsequently edited by Paul Radin. Bound, typed manuscript copies were available in the San Francisco Public Library and the Sutro Library. Although all but one of the tales is set in China, each seemed like a lens that helped focus on some facet of Chinese life in America. It was this material that I chose to retell. I combined some stories together; others were allowed to stand on their own.

Tricksters

There is a stereotype of the passive, quiet Chinese still being perpetuated in fiction and nonfiction. However, the history of the southern Chinese is full of feuds and rebellions. No matter how docile they might have appeared when in America, the old-time Chinese seemed to love the stories about tricksters. Still immensely popular are the stories about the Monkey King whose wit enabled a monk to bring sacred scripture from India.

Keeping one's wits could save one's life. And perhaps when someone described a particularly clever strategem like the one that the boy used to fool a monster like Dagger Claws, who appears in ''Bedtime Snacks,'' the listeners might have more confidence in themselves when it came to dealing with employers, labor contractors, storekeepers, and so on. The original tale, however, was far gorier and earthier.

Many animal fables, like ''Natural Enemies,'' explain why things are—usually at the expense of someone else. Of course, such tales are common to all cultures—and, according to Wolf-ram Eberhard, there are analogues in the Near East to one of the versions of the tale. However, this tale of the cat and the dog fits particularly into a genre of old Chinese tales that speak about predestination.

In the middle of the nineteenth century, the mortality rate could be as high as one in three dying, and yet the men came, to endure hardship, loneliness, and even persecution to send money home to their families back in China. Later times might change the type of troubles in America, but the troubles remained.

So "Natural Enemies" is more than an origin fable. It also reaffirms a certain world order that can include long hours for small wages, separation from the family, and whatever tribulations a man or woman might face.

As a way of breaking out of an economic trap or simply as a means of recreation, some Chinese will try their luck. Although not every Chinese gambles, every family would probably have had a black sheep like the rascally Chung of "The Professor of Smells." However, not every black sheep would have his wits and luck.

Bedtime Snacks

WHEN SHAKEY HEARD THE THUMP on the roof, he jerked his head up to stare at the ceiling. "What was that?"

His greedy little brother had already picked out the biggest bowl of rice. "It's just some old cat. Why are you such a coward?"

Shakey had gotten his nickname because every strange noise and shadow frightened him. Even so, he didn't see it that way. "I'm not a coward. I'm just cautious."

"That's good," their mother said, "but you go too far sometimes." She opened the door. "I'm going to visit some friends, so your Auntie will come to baby-sit."

Shakey put a finger to his lips. "Shh, Momma. You never know who might be listening."

"I think you're safe enough, dear; but even so, don't open to anyone but Auntie." Mother closed the door.

Up on the roof, the monster, Dagger Claws, merely smiled and waited.

Meanwhile, as Shakey lowered the crossbar across the door inside the house, his little brother mocked him. "Scaredy-cat, scaredy-cat."

Shakey sat down next to his little brother. "If you listened to your head more than your belly, you'd be scared too."

The two brothers had finished their meals and were washing the dishes when their elderly Auntie came to the door. Instantly Dagger Claws leaped down and killed the poor old woman with one swipe of her big claws.

When he heard the thud outside, Shakey was so scared that he dropped a rice bowl. It cracked on the floor; but he ignored the pieces. "Who's . . . who's there?" he called.

"Just your Auntie," Dagger Claws said in a high voice.

Crunch, crunch, crunch. Her big jaws munched on poor Auntie's bones.

Although he had already finished his dinner, the little brother was still hungry. One bowl of rice and a few vegetables were not enough for him. "Are you eating something good, Auntie?"

"Chestnuts," Dagger Claws lied. "Luscious, crisp chestnuts."

"Let me have some." The little brother ran to the door and lifted the bar.

Dagger Claws gobbled down the rest of poor old Auntie. "Only if you go to bed right now and put out the candle."

Shakey threw himself at the door before his little brother could open it. He was so scared that his teeth were chattering. "W-wh-y?"

"It hurts your poor old Auntie's eyes." Dagger Claws hurriedly put on Auntie's dress. She wanted two tasty little boys for her dessert.

The younger boy ran over to the big red candle to blow it out. Shakey darted after him and grabbed hold of his eager little brother. "But I don't like the dark, Auntie."

Dagger Claws scratched at the door. Her sharp claws left grooves in the wood. "Shame on you! You're a big boy now. Well, if you won't be nice to me, I won't be nice to you. No bedtime snacks."

"No, don't do that," the little brother said, and blew out the candle before Shakey could stop him.

The instant she saw the light go out underneath the door, Dagger Claws kicked it open with a bang. Shakey was so startled that he let go of his little brother.

For a moment, the moonlight silhouetted Dagger Claws. They saw nothing wrong because she looked like a round woman in a dress. Then she stepped in and shut the door so it was black inside the house. "Now get in bed, boys."

Shakey tried to get hold of his little brother, but he was already groping his way through the dark over to his sleeping mat.

"I'm over here, Auntie," the little brother called.

Dagger Claws stumbled blindly through the house. "Where?"

"Here, Auntie. Right here," the little brother said eagerly.

Dagger Claws followed the voice right to the sleeping mats. The next moment she had begun her own little snack. *Crunch, crunch, crunch.*

Shakey listened to Dagger Claws smack her lips and munch away happily. Shivering, he asked, "Little brother?"

Someone grunted in the darkness.

Shakey was so frightened that he could not move. "Is that you, little brother?" Shakey asked.

"He's busy eating his chestnuts," Dagger Claws said.

Crunch. Crunch. Crunch.

When Dagger Claws was almost finished, she called to Shakey, "Where are you? There's plenty of crisp, luscious chestnuts for everyone."

But Shakey was still so scared that he hunted for an excuse to stay where he was. "Aren't you thirsty?"

Both Auntie and the little brother had been rather salty, so Dagger Claws said, "I am a little thirsty."

"I'll get you a drink, Auntie," he offered.

Dagger Claws settled back. "What a sweet little boy." After a drink of water, she would have her third and last course.

Shakey forced himself to be calm. Hardly daring to breathe, he took a step. Then he took another and almost slipped on the wet floor. He tried not to think about why the floor was wet. He took a third step. The crunching began again. He looked neither to the right nor the left. Instead, he kept his eyes right on the door.

When he was outside, Shakey lowered the bucket into the well. Then he backed away. "Auntie, the bucket is too heavy. Come and help me."

"Just a moment. The moonlight hurts my eyes too." Dagger Claws rummaged around blindly until she found a basket. She dumped out the rice that was inside and put it over her head. Then she hid her big paws inside the sleeves of the dress. When she stepped outside the house, she could still see through the sides of the basket.

Shakey could not see her fangs or her paws, but he could see the strange tail that stuck out from under the dress. It whipped around in excitement. Then he knew Auntie was really a monster. It was too late to save Auntie or his little brother. He would be lucky to save himself.

It was a funny thing, but now that Shakey's worst fears were real, he wasn't scared anymore. Waiting had been the hardest part.

"There, Auntie." He pointed at the well.

Dagger Claws bent over the well. With her paws still inside her sleeves, she began to pull at the bucket's rope. "A strong boy like you can't lift a little bucket like this?"

Shakey ran to the well and shoved Dagger Claws with all his strength. With a screech, the monster fell headfirst down the well.

She landed with a big splash. Water rose up the well and crashed around the sides.

"I'll fix you!" she shrieked. She sank her long, hard claws into the sides of the well. *Thunk. Thunk.* She pulled herself out of the water. "I'll start with your toes first so you can watch me eat you." Slowly she began to climb up the sides. "You can run. You can hide. But I'll find you."

Shakey knew he didn't have much time. He picked up a long bamboo pole that lay next to the well and tied a big block of stone to the pole.

Dagger Claws was almost out of the well when Shakey lifted the long, heavy pole and swung the free end.

Dagger Claws dodged but some of the blows struck her. That only made her even angrier. "Just for that, I'm going to take you to my cave," she growled. "And I'm going to eat you slowly. One piece a day."

But Shakey kept poking and swinging at her until Dagger Claws lifted one paw and caught the bamboo pole. Her claws sank deep into the wood. "Hah! I've got your little stick now."

As she yanked at the pole, Shakey let go so that the pole went into the well and the stone followed the pole. Dagger Claws stared at the stone that fell past her.

Then the stone was pulling the pole after it. Too late, Dagger Claws tried to let go of the pole, but her sharp claws were embedded in its sides. Still holding the pole, Dagger Claws was yanked from the wall of the well.

Stone, pole, and monster splashed into the water, but this time Dagger Claws followed the stone down through the water. Down, down, down to the bottom of the well where she drowned.

They buried Shakey's little brother and Auntie and capped the well. And after that, when Shakey's mother visited friends, Shakey always went along with her.

Natural
Enemies

A LONG TIME AGO THERE WAS an old man who lived in a house down a city alley. High walls hid it from view. He had no family and his only company was a cat and dog.

He never went out to work. He didn't even go out to buy food. No one ever visited him. Naturally, everyone was very curious. But one thief was especially curious.

One night he snuck into a neighbor's courtyard and peeked over the walls. He saw a wonderful garden full of strange stones and waterfalls. In the center of the garden was a house fancy enough for an emperor.

The curious thief climbed over the wall and stole through the garden and into the house. The inside of the house was filled with fine furniture and antiques. Finally, he found the old man in the dining room. Tall pillars of red lacquer ran the length of the room. Gold covered the carvings on

13

the sides of the pillars. On the beams of the ceiling were painted different scenes of China.

The table and chairs were carved from rare purple woods. The old man sat in one chair with both a cat and a dog balanced on his lap. But there were neither plates of food on the table nor any servants to serve them.

The old man smiled at the dog. "And what do you want to eat tonight?"

The dog gave a bark and the old man nodded. "I thought so." He picked up a long slender ivory wand. The stem curved upward to a carved lotus. "As you like it, as I like it, I would like some beef stew."

A big golden bowl of beef stew popped into the air above the table and landed with a clank in front of the dog. The smell was delicious, and he happily began to wolf down his food.

"And what do you want?" the old man asked his cat. The cat merely licked her paws. "The same as usual, I suppose." The old man wished on the wand, and a big steaming carp appeared before the cat. With a disgusted look at the dog, the cat began to eat daintily.

Then the old man wished up his dinner on the wand. There were precious plates of gold encrusted with jewels and bowls carved from solid pieces of jade. But after the old man had drunk his wine, he gave a big yawn. "I think it's time for bed."

He wished the dirty plates all away, and then he and his two pets headed into the bedroom where he lay down on a big four-poster bed covered with silk and pearls. The dog and cat raced for the bed; but though the dog could run faster, the cat could leap higher. She got to the head of the bed first so the dog had to go to the foot.

"Leave some room for me," the old man laughed. He eased in between his two jealous pets. Soon the three were fast asleep.

The thief waited patiently until the old man and his pets had begun to snore. Then he snuck into the room and stole the wand.

The next morning, the old man woke and found his wand was missing. He hid his face in his hands and wept. "I'm ruined. Ruined! And I'm too old to go looking for the thief."

But then he felt something wet on the backs of his hands and he looked up to see that it was his cat and dog licking him. He put his hand on the dog. "Will you be my strong legs and go find him?" The dog's big tongue licked his hand again.

The old man looked at his cat. "Will you be my clever mind and get the wand?" And the cat's small tongue tickled his other hand.

The two loyal pets left the old man. They looked all over China. They lived by their skills and their wits. The dog sniffed around in alleys for things that people threw out. Sometimes, he had to fight the other beggars. But the dog was big and strong so he always won. He always shared his meals with the cat.

The cat learned how to leap up through kitchen windows and steal food. Often she would eat most of it inside the house. Then she would bring the leftovers to the dog.

Eventually, the two animals heard of a rich man who

had appeared out of nowhere. A broad, swift river separated them from his house. "You're strong enough to bear me," the cat said. "You carry me."

"But don't dig in your claws," the dog warned and crouched. The cat leaped onto his back, and the dog slipped into the river. The water was so cold and swift that the dog soon grew tired.

"I can't do it," the dog groaned.

"Yes, you can," the cat urged. "Think of home. Think of hot meals and soft silk."

So the dog went on until he climbed out exhausted on the opposite bank. "Now for the wand," the cat said. She wasn't tired at all and sped up the hill.

"Wait for me," the dog called and, shaking himself off, trotted after the cat.

But the cat did not want to wait for the big, slow dog. She dashed ahead impatiently. By now she was an expert at sneaking into houses. She crept silently into the villa. When she heard footsteps, she ducked behind a vase.

The thief strode by in a robe of silk embroidered with gold. Around his neck hung the wand on a golden chain. But he was not as careless as the old man. Two guards accompanied him at all times.

Going outside, the cat just stopped the dog from blundering inside. "We'll have to use both your strength and my wits to get the wand," she explained.

"Anything for the master," the dog promised.

They waited until the thief went for a walk in his garden. The dog suddenly darted out from under a bush and past the two startled guards and leaped on the thief, knocking him over.

"Stop him," the thief shouted frantically. The two guards could not use their swords because they might hurt their employer. Instead, they tried to pull the dog away.

While the dog was fighting for his life, the cat shot in like a small streak of fur. Perching on the rich man's chest, she pressed her paws against the wand. When the thief reached for the wand, the cat bit his hand so he snatched it back.

Silently, the cat wished, "As you like it, as I like it, I would like to be back home with the wand."

As the cat began to fade from sight, the dog barked at her. "Wait for me, wait for me."

But the cat vanished from sight.

The next moment, she was back in the old man's bedroom. The old man lay in a ragged robe on a simple straw mat. He had sold everything else to pay his debts. Through the window, the cat could see that the garden itself had fallen into ruin.

"Thank Heaven, you've come back," the old man said. "I was getting so lonely. I don't care whether you brought back the wand."

But the cat picked up the wand in her mouth and brought it over to the old man. Gently she let it drop into the old man's lap.

"You did bring it back!" the old man cried out. "You blessed animal." He held out his hand. "But where's our other friend? Didn't he come with you? Or did he get tired and go off on his own?"

The cat simply looked up at the old man, and the old man reached his own hasty conclusions. While the old man cursed the dog, the cat curled up on his knees. Both the lap and the magic were hers now.

The old man wished the thief to his just reward and then restored the house. But he never gave another thought to the dog until months later. Suddenly there was a familiar barking outside the gates.

The old man opened them to see his tired, dusty dog. One ear was torn, and he was badly scratched. The old man frowned. "Now that the cat's made everything right, you've decided to come back. Well, it's too late."

The cat, fat and sleek, strolled up behind the old man. "Tell him, tell him," the dog barked angrily.

But the cat merely began to lick itself. And then the old man had shut the gates on the dog. "Stop making so much noise," the old man shouted over the gates. "Or I'll send you to the Himalayas."

The dog slunk away so the cat had the old man all to herself. But all dogs remember the cat's treachery, and dogs have hated cats ever since then.

The Professor of Smells

ONCE THERE WAS A GAMBLER NAMED CHUNG. He would bet on anything. He would bet on the weather. He would bet on how many cockroaches were in a cupboard. He once even bet that the sun would set in the east.

His poor wife used to pull at her hair because of his gambling. She worried so much that she yanked her hair into spikes.

One day, he came home without any money. He found his wife in their small vegetable patch. Her ducks waddled around her feet, quacking and eating the insects that her hoe turned up. "I was winning," he said to his wife. "But I made just one bad bet. Give me some of your egg money and I'll double it for you."

She shook her head. "As they say, 'Don't fill the jar when it's cracked.'"

Chung promised desperately, "If I don't win this time, I'll give up gambling for good."

His wife believed him because she wanted to, and went and got her money. Each cash was a round coin with a square hole through which a string had been run. Although she had saved a year to get two strings of a hundred cash each, she gave them both to him.

He went straight back to the wine shop where his friends were gambling. By the door was a picture of the Pure White Lord. He stood in rich robes and held a pair of dice in his hand.

In front of the picture was a small, narrow table on which sat a cup of dirt. He lit an incense stick and thrust it into the dirt beside all the other burning sticks.

The owner was standing in front of a large table. His hands rested on a big bowl that was turned over. He moved the bowl around in quick circles so that the beans inside rattled against the sides. "Who'll bet? Who'll bet? Better to be wealthy than healthy. Better to be rich than digging a ditch. Who'll bet? Who'll bet?"

Chung found a spot on a bench and slapped his two strings of cash down. He stared hard at the bowl. He felt magical and powerful all at the same time. He felt like he could see the beans inside. He knew just how many were there. "One," he declared.

The owner nodded and finished taking all the bets. Then he lifted the bowl and with a single chopstick drew the beans away, four at a time.

When only half the beans were gone, Chung's experienced eyes saw that there would be three beans left. He had lost all of his wife's egg money. "Chung," he reprimanded himself, "you were so sure. Where did you go wrong?"

One of Chung's friends was a big man with messy hair. Although the big man never seemed to work, he always had money and he always had good luck. He had doubled his money. "Chung, why don't you just give your money away?" He laughed as he jingled his winnings in the air.

It was a magical, musical sound to Chung. He didn't care about his promise to his wife. "Chung," he said to himself, "you just have to squeeze some more money out of your wife."

On his way home, he thought and thought about different plans when he happened to pass by the coffin maker's. As he heard the sound of the saw, he had an idea.

When the coffin maker saw Chung, he grunted. "I don't have any money. And even if I did, I wouldn't loan it to you."

But Chung scooped up a handful of shavings. "May I?"

Puzzled, the coffin maker shrugged. "Be my guest."

Chung sprinkled the wood shavings all over himself and then ran into his house. "If you give me money, you'll be the happiest woman in the world." He lifted his wife up and whirled her around in a circle.

"Put me down." She slapped at his shoulders until he obeyed. Then she smoothed out her blouse. "No more money for gambling."

"That's all done." Chung dusted the shavings from his hair and shoulders. "Sawing wood is so much more fun."

"It is?" the wife asked in surprise.

"I lost the money, so I left. But then I saw a new house being built. When I stopped to watch, the carpenter invited me to help." He shoved his arm forward and then drew it back as if he were sawing. "I had so much fun that the carpenter said I could become his apprentice. I just have to pay him one string of cash."

The wife looked around their barren house. They slept on mats under a moth-eaten quilt. They now had only one pot to their name and two cracked dishes. "But we don't have any money."

"It's a shame," Chung sighed. "The fee is usually higher, but the carpenter liked me."

"We mustn't waste this chance." The wife looked sadly at her ducks. "My ducks are almost like pets. And we sell the eggs for money."

"It's just temporary. I'll sell them. Then with my wages, I'll buy your ducks right back," the gambler promised.

As soon as he had sold the ducks, he went right back to the wine shop and plunked his money down. "I know it's one this time," he said.

But the number of beans was two.

Chung stood there in a daze. "That's impossible."

His big friend tapped him on the shoulder. "Are you going to set up house there, or are you going to let a player get into the game?"

Chung sadly stepped outside and stopped in front of the pawnshop. He finally realized the enormity of what he had done. "Chung," he said to himself, "you're rotten through and through. You've taken everything from your wife— even her pet ducks. I wouldn't blame her if she left you now. Why did you have to gamble?"

He walked through the village, desperately trying to think

of some story that would fool her. As he wandered by a tinsmith, he saw something flash in the dirt. He bent hopefully, thinking that it might be money, but it was only an old piece of tin about the length of his finger.

"Chung, maybe you could disguise yourself." He playfully put the tin over his nose. To his surprise, it fit perfectly and that gave him another idea. He went back into the wine shop and borrowed a knife. With the knife he punched two holes into the piece of the tin. Then he got some string from the wine shop and tied the tin over his nose.

Sneaking home, he saw his wife at the stove. Rice bubbled on the stove. Next to it was a duck's egg.

His wife was cutting up some vegetables. But she cut too fast. Giving a little cry, she lifted her knife and sucked at the cut on her finger.

Chung quietly left his house. Then he came back inside and said loudly, "Woman, what do you have for a hungry working man?"

"How is my carpenter?" The wife turned around happily. But the smile left her face. Instead, she just stared. "What happened to your nose?"

"I've found a better profession." He tapped a nail against the tin so that it rang. "I'm a professor of smells."

The wife folded her arms skeptically. "You lost all my money and all my ducks. I trusted you."

"No, no, I can smell out anything." He pointed to the dinner that lay covered up by lids. "My educated nose tells me that you have cooked rice, an omelet, and vegetables for our dinner. Am I right?"

His wife snorted. "Anyone could smell food in a kitchen."

But then he sniffed the air first to his left and then to his right. "I smell blood." He looked at her accusingly. "What an odd sort of dinner?!"

His wife held up her cut finger. "I cut my finger just now. That's what you must have smelled."

He turned in profile. "I told you this was an educated nose." He clinked a fingernail against the tin. "I can find anything by smell."

"Then you can find lost things?" the wife asked in delight.

Chung was so busy congratulating himself on his cleverness that he didn't think. "Anything," he swore.

His wife served his dinner and went outside. As Chung ate, he could hear his wife boasting about her husband's new profession to their neighbors. She added, "For a small fee, he will find anything you've lost."

Chung nearly choked on a mouthful of rice.

"Even my great-aunt's thimble?" a woman asked.

Chung knocked himself on his head. "Chung, you've gotten yourself into an even worse mess." Outside, his proud wife was taking down a list of lost objects that he was to find.

The next day, the professor of smells made a big show of sniffing the air. He walked all around their village. Then he went out the gates and sat down in the orchard. The tin hurt his nose, so he took it off and set it on a rock. It would not be long before everyone knew he was a liar. Then the whole village would make fun of him, and his wife would be angry.

Suddenly a big magpie landed and tried to pick up the

tin. Chung waved his hand irritably. "Leave me *some*thing." The magpie took off.

As Chung watched it rise through the orchard trees, he had another thought. If the magpie liked bright things, maybe the magpie had stolen other bright things. He took out the list and looked at it. The missing items were all shiny things.

Picking up his tin nose, he raced up the slope after the magpie. Sometimes he tripped over rocks, sometimes over tree roots; but the determined gambler always stumbled to his feet and kept the magpie in sight. Finally, the magpie roosted in a tall tree.

Climbing the tree, he found the magpie's nest near a hole in the tree. Putting his hand inside, he pulled out a thimble. Eagerly he took out all the other missing items.

Once on the ground, he buried each item in the orchard and carefully memorized their locations. Then he went back into the village, again sniffing. "I'm close. I'm close!" And when he had gathered a small crowd, he led them back to the orchard.

Sniffing the air, he ran back and forth among the fruit trees. Finally, he pointed at one neighbor. "Your thimble is here."

The woman skeptically dug into the dirt and straightened in amazement. She held the thimble up for everyone to see. "This is it! But how did it get here?"

Chung shrugged. "I'm a professor of smells, not of reasons."

One by one, he found the other items to the growing amazement of the crowd. His proud wife collected the fees;

and they returned to the village and bought back her ducks.

Soon his fame spread throughout the district. Then one day a sedan chair came to their house. Out stepped a man in expensive robes. He bowed to the startled wife. "I must see the professor of smells. I've lost my prize pig."

The wife tilted back her head regally. "I'll see if he's free."

As soon as she was in the house, she rushed over to the sleeping mat and woke him. "There's a rich man outside who wants you to find his pig."

No magpie would have stolen a pig. "I'm too tired," Chung said.

His wife poked him in the chest. "Professors aren't supposed to be temperamental."

Chung hated to disappoint his wife. "I could listen to him, I suppose," Chung said, and put on his tin nose.

When he went outside, the rich man bowed. "I was going to breed new stock with this special pig. Now I've lost her. Please, Professor, won't you help me?"

Chung was going to refuse politely, but his wife stepped in front of him. "The professor," she said haughtily, "is a busy man. His skills are in much demand."

The rich man bowed again. "I'm desperate." He took a pouch from his sleeve and held it out. "I hate to insult him with money. However, these gold coins will meet some of his expenses. Once he finds the pig, he's welcome to a second pouch."

Before Chung could stop her, his wife had taken the pouch. "And what does your pig look like?"

"She's all brown except for a white spot around her eye." The rich man drew a circle around his right eye.

When the rich man left, Chung's wife hugged him. "Everyone said you were worthless when we got married. But I knew. I had faith."

Chung did not have the heart to tell her the truth. But then he muttered to himself, "Chung, if a magpie didn't steel the pig, someone else might have." So he asked his wife for a little cash.

"You're not going to go back to gambling, are you?" his wife asked.

"No, but I need wine to sharpen my nose." He went to the wine shop. Once inside, he took off the tin nose and looked around until he saw his man.

Then he paid for a jar of warm wine. He did not drink at all. Instead, he sat down by his big friend. He kept filling the big man's cup. Soon the one big man was very drunk. He looked around the wine shop and then crooked a finger at Chung. "You're a good fellow. You just have the luck of a slug. You're welcome to a barbecue next week."

"I like pork," Chung said carefully.

The big robber slapped a hand on Chung's shoulder. "Then you're in luck. I've got the pig of all pigs for you. I found her in her own little house—just like she was a person. And the floor was all tile. I never saw the like."

Chung pretended to think a moment. Then he shook his head. "You don't know how long it's been since I've had pork, but I went to a wise old woman. She said I could only eat brown pigs with white circles around their eyes. I don't think there is any such animal."

The big robber slapped Chung on the back. "It must be this pig's destiny to be your dinner. That's the exact description of the animal I . . . uhh . . . found."

Chung realized this could only be the rich man's pig. He looked over at the picture of the Pure White Lord. "Help me," he begged the picture, "not for my sake but for my wife's. And I swear I won't ask for your help again."

"What did you say?" the big robber asked.

"Nothing." Chung counted out his cash. "I don't suppose you'd like a little game?"

"That'll be the easiest money I'll ever make." The robber grinned. He held up a hand. "Let's play scissors, paper, and rock."

They began to match hands, but the Pure White Lord must have wanted to get rid of Chung. This time Chung won and kept on winning. In no time, he had the robber's money and the pig too.

Then the professor of smells led the pig back to the grateful rich man and received the second pouch of gold.

Naturally, the fame of the professor of smells spread far and wide after that. Chung enjoyed his new reputation and the respect he now received, but his wife enjoyed it even more. "I knew he was special," his wife would boast to their neighbors. "And now everyone knows."

And Chung said to himself, "Chung, there isn't a better wife than her. If you're enjoying good times, it's for her merits—not yours."

So when his old friends would come around, he would refuse to go gambling with them.

But one day a company of soldiers marched into the village and straight to Chung's door. They set a sedan chair down and an official in elegant robes climbed out.

"Professor Chung," the official announced solemnly,

"word has reached His Imperial Highness of your special skills. He begs you to come to the capital right away. His jade seal has been lost. No document is official without it. The government is paralyzed. An army of soldiers and clerks has searched the palace; but they could find nothing now. Your country turns to you now in its hour of need. You must find the lost seal."

Chung, the gambler thought to himself, you're in for it now. And out loud he said, "It's impossible. I have no such talents."

"This is no time to be modest," his wife hissed at him.

The official tapped him with his fan. "Your wife is right. Anyway, you have no choice. His Imperial Highness summons you."

Chung clutched at his head and bowed. "You have to believe me. I'm telling the truth. I'm a fraud."

But the official signed to some soldiers. They picked up the protesting Chung and dumped him into a second chair.

All the way to the palace, Chung imagined what would happen. "Chung," he said to himself, "it's only fair if they torture you. You've been a cheat and a liar all your life. But then they'll punish your wife and all your kin and all your neighbors, and that isn't fair."

By the time they had reached the audience hall, he had scared himself thoroughly with such thoughts. He was so frightened that he walked straight up to the dragon throne. All the officials and soldiers stared in disbelief. Even the emperor was amazed.

One of his advisors pointed a finger at Chung. "Don't you know you're supposed to make three kowtows and nine bows? You should lose your head for such an insult."

But the emperor was intrigued. "He's either a fool or an extraordinary man."

Chung thought that this was his way out. "Well, if you don't want my help, I'll just leave." He turned on his heel and started to walk out.

The emperor quickly made up his mind. "Wait!" he called.

Chung faced the emperor again. "What is it now?"

The emperor flushed an angry red, but he swallowed his pride. "Professor Chung, you have forty days to prove your skills as an extraordinary man. In that time, you will either help me find my jade seal or I will help you find some manners." He smiled unpleasantly. "And you won't like your lessons."

Chung began that very hour to look all over the palace. It wasn't just one big building but dozens. Some were rooms where the emperor and his family stayed. Others were government offices and soldiers' barracks and quarters for the servants. There were even gardens and parks.

Chung went diligently through the rooms and over the grounds. Whenever anyone saw him, he would pretend to sniff the air vigorously. But by the thirty-ninth day, he had covered only half of the palace.

He slumped miserably against the wall and moaned. He knew he could not succeed where an army had failed. "Chung," he said out loud to himself, "you're done for. You can't fool the emperor anymore."

Now it so happened that one of the king's advisors happened to be in the hallway outside of the office. He stopped dead in his tracks and stared at Chung. It was the same advisor who had wanted Chung's head. "You can't prove a thing!" the advisor said.

"I was just talking to myself," Chung said.

"It's a bad habit." The advisor walked away hastily.

The gambler suddenly had a hunch, and this hunch was stronger than anything he had felt when he was gambling. "Chung, maybe the White Lord is taking pity on you still." He followed the advisor and found out his name was Chung just like his.

"Aha!" Chung said to himself.

The professor of smells nosed around the capital and found that the advisor lived as royally as a prince. He had a fancy palace of his own and an army of servants. "Aha and double aha! My namesake likes to live high on the hog," the professor of smells said.

Next the professor of smells went to some of the fancy gambling places and the expensive restaurants and antique dealers. The advisor owed everyone.

"Chung," he said to himself, "you're having a streak of luck. You might as well follow it out to its end."

He returned to the palace and started sniffing down one hallway and up another. When he found the advisor, he circled him, sniffing, snorting, and sneezing. "There's a smell of jade to you."

The advisor held up the jade ornaments that decorated his sash. "Of course, you idiot."

But the professor of smells went on smelling the advisor. "No, this has an inkish smell to it. Sort of a seal-ish scent."

The advisor gathered himself up stiffly. "You're imagining things."

Chung tapped the side of his nose with a loud clink.

"You doubted me, but this is no ordinary nose. It can smell out seals. It can smell out debts and even where they're from," and Chung named a half dozen places. "If I were the thief and I owed that much money, then I might be desperate enough to come up with a scheme. I might hold the imperial seal for ransom. Or I might sell it to some rival of the emperor's. Then they could get their decrees made official."

The advisor sank to his knees and bowed his head. "You truly are a professor of smells. Despite my debts, I still have a considerable fortune. You can have half of it if you can keep me from disgrace."

Chung felt like singing and dancing for joy. However, he managed to keep a stern face. "Well, since we have the same name, we must have the same ancestor some time back in the past. For his sake, bring the seal to me and then resign."

The advisor gratefully obeyed Chung's orders, and Chung buried the seal in one of the gardens under a magnolia tree.

The next day he marched straight into the audience hall. The emperor glared down at Chung. "I see you haven't learned any manners."

But Chung put up a hand for silence and began to sniff.

"What is it?" the emperor demanded.

"Quiet," Chung snapped. "All that talk distracted me last time." He walked right up the dais to the dragon throne and sniffed the emperor's fingers. Then he began to sniff the air. "Yes, Chung," he mumbled to himself, "that's it." Still sniffing the air, he ran out of the audience hall.

The emperor sat on his throne in astonishment. Then he

suddenly jumped to his feet. Raising the hem of his long gown, he looked around at his equally amazed court. "Let's see what this extraordinary man is up to." And he scampered after the professor of smells with the rest of the court close at his heels.

Mumbling to himself all the time, Chung led them on a merry chase through one building after another. He scuttled up stairs, leaped through windows, and climbed walls. The emperor and his court had quite forgotten their dignity now. Finally, when their elegant silk robes were all torn and dirty and they were panting like a blacksmith's bellows, Chung led them to the magnolia tree.

"It's the scent of the flowers that threw me off." He circled all around the tree and suddenly began digging in the spot where he had buried the jade seal. "And here the little devil is!"

Wiping it off, he presented it to the emperor. As the emperor took it, he stared down at the hole. "But how did it ever get there?"

Chung simply smiled. "Your Highness, I am a humble professor of smells—not of reasons."

"You must teach this talent to others," the emperor said.

"Alas, Your Majesty. I've strained my nose night and day in your service. I'm afraid it's quite used up." Chung removed his tin nose. "The professor of smells is no more."

Between the grateful emperor and his ex-advisor, Chung went home loaded down with wealth and fame. And he and his wife lived quite comfortably for the rest of their lives.

But he never gambled again. He knew that he had used up enough luck for a dozen professors of smells.

Fools

Tales about fools provide a counterpoint to trickster stories: We are never as clever as we think we are. As Walter de la Mare said: "Nonsense is simply wisdom turned upside down" and in certain situations—particularly in a strange country with a different culture—the fool becomes the wise man and vice versa. For all of the reason and logic of Confucian scholars, there was also a truth in the absurdities of Chuang Tzu, the butterfly philosopher, and the ch'an masters who gave birth to zen.

Quite often, the fool may be intelligent enough—just given to misinterpretation like the would-be gourmet and his eels in The Eel's Disguise. A person misinterprets on the basis of little or wrong information—a situation in which many newcomers, fresh off the boat, must have found themselves. There were surely jokes played at their expense by the old-timers or the native-born.

Then, too, the old-timers would have understood if you spoke of people with little luck; no matter how hard that person may try, he or she is bound to fail—as does the woman who is the child of calamity. I include a number of bad-luck stories— including details from the tale of the Kitchen God.

The underlying message to many stories is not to trust anyone or anything—neither baby-sitters nor even such innocent things as stones as in "The Ghost's Bride." If sitting on one back in China could lead to trouble, then America must have seemed twice as dangerous because of its many unknown variables. Ghosts' brides appeared not only in fiction but in fact as well, and a marriage was typical of the demands of the dead.

"The Butterfly Man" reminds us that even a smart person trips up occasionally. Many madmen and beggars are simply what they seem. It's the wise person who can tell the saint. (Nor was it uncommon in times of extreme suffering for men to go off to find work and send money home.)

The
Eel's
Disguise

A CERTAIN FOOL LIVED IN A FARAWAY VILLAGE. He was so foolish that his wife had to take care of everything. However, one day she had to stay in the fields. She called her husband over to her and pointed to two baskets of vegetables. "It's market day in the town. Take these straight to my cousin who lives there. Now repeat my orders."

"I'll go straight to your cousin," the fool mumbled.

"You let him do the selling," the wife instructed.

"Everyone thinks I'm an idiot," the fool grumbled. "I can do it."

"Maybe another time," the wife said calmly. She had heard the fool complain like this many times. "Today you let my cousin do everything. And what is it he's going to do?"

"Sell the vegetables."

"Good." The wife picked up a big hoe. "And once you have the money, buy something for our supper."

"What do you want?" the fool asked his wife.

The wife felt a little guilty for being so bossy, so she smiled. "Anything will do. Surprise me."

So the fool hung a basket at either end of a pole and then shouldered the pole. Outside the village walls, he skirted the pond where the village raised fish. Then he walked along the narrow paths past the fields until he reached the main road.

Other farmers were walking along with their loads balanced at either end of the long bamboo poles. They chatted with one another to pass the time. One man glanced at the fool's baskets. "You ought to get a lot for those big vegetables."

"And what should I buy for supper?" the fool asked.

The man thought a moment. "My brother works for a rich family. He says that eels are wonderful to eat."

"I've never had eels," the fool said. "No one in our village has."

"Then you're in for a treat," the man said. "Slice them up and fry them with a little ginger and a little soy sauce. It's a treat that can't be beat."

"I'll show my wife how clever I am. We'll have a fancy treat just like the rich folk." The fool hurried on, eager to buy those wonderful eels. When he got to town, he went straight to his wife's cousin. Although the cousin had been born on a farm, he had lived in the town for a long time and seemed quite worldly to the fool.

The cousin greeted the fool cheerfully and led him to the marketplace. It was a busy place with stalls that had every sort of sweet and fancy silks. Barbers were there with their sharp razors, and there was even a traveling black-smith with a small anvil. His hammer rang steadily as the farmers shouted to the passersby.

"Pork," announced one. "I've got pork from a pig fat as a buffalo!"

"Turnips sweet as pears!" another yelled. "Turnips sweet as pears!"

The cousin squeezed into a narrow space between the two farmers. "Now, now, two tiny people like you can make room for two more."

The farmer set down the pole and slid the baskets in front of the cousin. Then he leaned the pole against a convenient wall.

The cousin was a small man, but he had a big voice that boomed over the others. "Fresh vegetables. Big, leafy vegetables. Fried or boiled. Sliced or whole. It doesn't matter. They'll put the juice into you."

He had no trouble attracting customers and in time he sold all the vegetables at a good price. He handed the money to the fool. "Your wife should be pleased."

The fool handed back a tip to thank the cousin. "She told me to buy something for supper."

The cousin spread his hands. "Take your pick. You've got the best of the whole district all around you."

The fool, though, had just one thought in his head. "Eels. I want eels."

"Wouldn't you rather have pork?" The cousin laughed.

"I know what I want," the fool insisted.

"What did your wife want?" the cousin asked.

"She left it up to me," the fool said. "And I want eels.

Cut them up and cook them with ginger and soy sauce. Then you've got a treat that can't be beat."

"Aren't you the gourmet?" the cousin wondered, but he led the fool over to a cart.

The merchant was shouting, "I've got fish. I've got squid. I've got oysters."

"What about eels?" the cousin asked.

"If it swims, crawls, or just sits in the water, I've got it." The merchant showed them a bucket. Three eels coiled at the bottom.

Once the fool saw what eels were, he wasn't so sure he wanted them. "No one said they looked like worms."

The merchant sized up the fool in a glance. "And I took you for a man of the world. Anyone can see that these eels are luscious enough for an emperor's table."

The fool puffed himself up. "Of course, I know that. I was just making an observation."

The merchant leaned over and said in a low voice, "Well, then, you also know that eels aren't for common folk. It takes a special person to appreciate them."

The cousin bargained with the merchant until the fool had bought the bucket of eels.

Leaving the basket and pole with the cousin, the fool marched happily out of town. He thought to himself, the village will be impressed by our special meal. Then I dare anyone to call me a fool.

But he couldn't help noticing how muddy the eels looked. My wife, he said to himself, isn't as sophisticated as I am. I'd better clean them.

When he reached the village, he went straight to the pond. The fish swam like a dark cloud beneath the water.

They rose hungrily when they saw him. But when they realized the fool wasn't going to feed them, they drifted back toward the bottom.

Kneeling by the pond, he dipped the bucket into the water. Immediately, an eel wriggled out of the bucket. "Come back here." The husband snatched desperately at the eel, but it easily curved over his hand and disappeared at the bottom of the pond.

Even as he was trying to grab the first one, the second eel slipped out of the bucket. "Not you too." He tried to pull it back into the bucket, but the second eel also got away.

Hurriedly, the fool lifted the bucket out of the pond, but the third eel slithered over the lip of the bucket and splashed into the pond. The fool stared into the empty bucket.

"Oh no," he groaned. "I'm in for it now. I spent all that money on eels, and now I have nothing to show for it. What will the village say? What will my wife say?"

He set the bucket down and put his nose close to the water. But there wasn't a ripple from their supper. Straightening up, he saw a turtle by the pond. Its face was turned up toward the sun.

The fool thought the turtle's head looked just like an eel's. "Hah! You can't trick me with that disguise."

He tiptoed around the pond, but he hadn't paid attention to the sun. His shadow fell across the turtle. Instantly, the turtle woke up and tried to dive into the water. But it was too slow. The fool snatched up the turtle. "You outsmarted yourself that time. You can't move fast enough in that heavy costume." Keeping both hands on the turtle, he paraded into the village.

"What are you doing?" people asked him.

"I'm going to have eel for supper," he said proudly. "With ginger and soy sauce, you can't beat it for a treat."

When he entered his house, he called to his wife. "Come and see the special treat I bought for our supper."

His wife frowned. "No one eats mud turtles."

The fool held the turtle out toward her. "Don't you know an eel when you see one?"

The wife knocked on the turtle's shell. "And what's this?"

The fool puffed himself up. "Any fool can see what it is—his vest."

His wife sighed. "And you're not just any fool."

"I stopped at the pond to wash the eels, but they got away. However, this one thought he could disguise himself." He rapped a knuckle on the shell. "But I'd know him even if he wore a beard and a scholar's robes!"

The wife realized then what had happened. "I told you to surprise me, and you certainly did."

And though her husband had wasted a good deal of their money, she laughed because there was nothing else she could do. Then she told the fool to bring the turtle back to the pond. And that night, they dined on rice and vegetables.

But he stayed the fool to the rest of the village.

The
Child
of
Calamity

ONCE THERE WAS A WOMAN with no luck. Her husband and almost all her children had died while she was still young. Only one daughter survived to help her.

Finally, her daughter said, "No one has this much bad luck. Let's ask some priests to get rid of it."

On the appointed day the priests arrived in robes and caps. Inside the unfortunate woman's house, they set up an altar and burned big red candles and dozens of incense sticks. With their prayer books, they tried to pray the bad luck away. Then, with their brushes and scrolls, they tried to write it away. Finally, with their swords of peach wood, they tried to scare it away.

Suddenly one of the priests clutched his throat and dropped to the floor. The others immediately stopped and examined their fallen brother.

"He's dead," one priest said. With a shake of his head, he straightened up and addressed the woman. "I'm sorry. Each person only can hold so much luck. It's like a pitcher of water. The larger the pitcher, the more it can hold. Some people can have lots of luck; others can only have a small amount. Like you. Blessings could rain down from heaven, and nothing would change. You were born to be a child of calamity."

"I've never been one to give up," the woman vowed.

She went on trying to feed herself and her daughter, but the earth grudged her the most miserable plants. Although her daughter did not complain, the woman could not stand to watch her slowly starve to death. Reluctantly, she let another family adopt her daughter. "One of these days," she promised her tearful daughter, "Heaven will take pity on us."

Then she cut herself a small stick to beat off the dogs and got a bowl. She hid each up a sleeve so that no one would see her when she left the village. She did not take them out until she was in another district where no one would know her. Once there, she began to beg for her food.

She wandered and suffered for a long time. Even so, no matter how desperate she was, she never stole. I won't hurt another soul, she told herself.

Ten years went by. The daughter had married a merchant who took her to another province. She was surprised one day when she thought she saw her mother begging in the streets.

"Mercy," the old woman called out. "Mercy." She held out her bowl hopefully to people.

Not wanting to embarrass her mother, the daughter baked

two cakes and in one cake she put a silver coin. Then she had a servant bring the cakes to her mother.

The mother was just about to eat them when she saw an old beggar woman who could not even walk. Instead, she crawled on all fours with her stick in one hand and her bowl hanging around her neck. And there were worms in her hair.

"Here," the woman said, and gave one of the cakes to the old beggar woman.

"Heaven will bless you, child," the old beggar woman said tearfully.

The old beggar woman's thanks made the woman uncomfortable. "It's all right," she said, and left before the old beggar woman could bite into the cake. The other beggar, of course, got the coin because it was just as the priest said: The woman was a child of calamity.

Eventually, though, she grew tired of the road and went to her brother's village.

Stopping by a stream, she began to clean herself up. Immediately, children began to point and laugh at her. "This isn't a show," she said.

The children promptly picked up stones and began throwing them at her.

"Stop that," a man ordered. She was relieved to see it was her brother.

When she identified herself, her brother hugged her. "We thought you were dead."

He took her up to his house, where his wife frowned at him. "I would never go back to my old village," his wife said. "She's a disgrace."

The woman held her head up proudly. "I've done nothing to be ashamed of. I've hurt no one, and I always shared what little I had. One day Heaven will reward me."

"And in the meantime we'll have to feed you," her sister-in-law sniffed.

The woman would have liked nothing better than to turn around and leave, but her brother was her last hope. "I'm too old to beg food from strangers. No one would want me as a slave. Let me stay here."

"There's no room," her sister-in-law said.

The brother blushed a bright red, but he didn't dare contradict his wife. "Maybe not in the house. But there's the stall with the water buffalo."

Her sister-in-law looked the woman up and down. "She's filthy. Heaven knows what diseases she has. Our water buffalo could catch something from her and die. Then where would we be? We need the money we get renting the buffalo out to plow."

The woman got down on her knees and touched her forehead against the dirt. "I'll pull the plow myself. Give me a corner in the courtyard. Let me have the scraps the pigs don't want."

The brother looked at his wife helplessly, but the wife pulled the beggar woman to her feet and shoved her out the door. "Go on. I know your kind. You're just too lazy to work."

The rest of the village had gathered in the meantime. They were waiting outside the gates to point and laugh.

It was all the woman could take. She fell to her knees and cried, but her tears only made the people laugh all the louder. Turning her face toward Heaven, she held out her hands. "Have mercy on me."

And Heaven finally heard and took pity on her. A silver coin fell from the sky and landed with a clink in front of her. The villagers immediately fell silent, awed by the spectacle.

"Thank you," the woman began gratefully when a second coin fell. Then a third. Then a fourth.

"That's hers, that's hers," her sister-in-law said. She fell to her knees and began picking up the coins. "Ow." A coin struck her on the shoulder. She put a hand up to the bruised spot when a coin hit her hand. "Ow."

The beggar woman put both her hands over her head. "Ow. Ow." Hastily, her sister-in-law scrambled out of the way.

Silver coins rained down from Heaven all around the woman until she was buried to her waist. Still the coins fell. "I can't move," she cried as the coins clinked and rang all around her.

"She'll be buried alive." Her brother tried to force his way through the shower of coins, but he had to retreat.

The beggar woman became afraid then. Maybe her brother was right. The coins crushed her sides. She couldn't breathe. "I don't want your money," she gasped.

Instantly, the coins began to rise from the ground. They swept skyward in a silver column to vanish into the sky.

The sister-in-law got down on all fours again. "You idiot. There's not even a single piece left."

As her brother knelt beside her, the beggar woman glanced up at Heaven. She knew that she could never expect such miraculous fortune again. "The priest was right," she finally admitted. "I'm a true child of calamity. All I can do is die."

The brother helped his bruised sister to her feet. "But if

Heaven took pity once, then so should we." He looked at his wife.

And after what she had seen, his wife didn't argue with him.

So he led his sister back inside his house, and she stayed with him until she died.

The
Ghost's
Bride

"COME BACK RIGHT AWAY," the mother ordered her daughter.

"I will," the girl promised, and she went straight to the next village and did the errand for her mother. But on her way back, the girl began to drag her feet lazily. It was a warm, sunny day, and the girl did not want to go back right away to her chores. So, instead, she sat down on a large, flat stone by a stream and took off her shoes.

At first she splashed her feet happily in the cool water. But then gradually it became harder and harder to wriggle her toes. She thought the water might be too cold so she lifted her feet out to let the sun warm them.

When they still felt stiff, she tried to rub her feet, but she felt nothing. Worse, her ankles and calves were also numb. Worried, she swung her legs from the stone and tried to stand up.

She swayed on her feet, suddenly feeling very tired. She thought about lying down on the stone. It was so pleasant here, and her mean mother worked her too hard. She just needed to rest a moment more.

But in the back of her mind, she felt uneasy. She tried to walk back to her village, but she could barely move her legs. By the time she reached the village gates, her legs were as stiff as sticks.

She collapsed in the dirt, calling for help. The other villagers heard her and carried her to her house. Her anxious mother put her to bed and did everything she could think of, but the girl's legs became useless. The girl could no longer even walk.

"Did you fall down?" her mother asked.

The girl began to cry. "No."

Puzzled, her mother shook her head. "Something must have happened. You went straight there and back again?"

Through her tears, the girl mumbled, "You'll just scold me."

Her mother stroked her hair just as she had when her daughter was small. "I do scold you. Maybe too much. But that's because I love you."

The girl sniffed. "Well, I did take a little rest."

Her mother kept on stroking her hair. "Where?"

"By the stream near a big flat stone," the girl said.

The worried mother made her daughter comfortable and then retraced her daughter's steps. She even found the stone and the stream. Everything seemed normal.

Completely puzzled now, the mother went to a wise old woman in the next village. The old woman knew how to talk to ghosts.

The wise old woman was laying bundles of herbs out to dry in front of her hut. When the mother told her of their troubles, the wise old woman just shook her head and clicked her tongue. "She sat on the lap of a dead man. Now he wants her for his bride."

"She only sat on a stone," the mother wondered.

"Long ago a farmer died when he was young. A stone marked his grave, but the stone fell over long ago." The old woman went on sadly with her chores. "Beneath the stone lies the man, and beneath the stone that man waits."

But the mother was not about to give up her daughter without a fight. She went back to the stone with bowls of food and a jar of wine for the ghost. Then she burned special paper money and begged the man to leave her daughter alone.

It was late afternoon by the time she started back for home. Her shadow stretched far behind her like a long, thin puppet. Suddenly she had the feeling that she wasn't alone. When the mother looked behind her, she saw two shadows. The second shadow was that of a man.

"Go away. I don't want a ghost for a son-in-law." She picked up the nearest stone and threw it at the second shadow, and the shadow disappeared.

The mother thought to herself, Maybe I can drive him away from my girl.

So that night the determined mother sat down in a chair and kept watch. In her lap was her big kitchen cleaver. When the shadow appeared on the wall, she waved the cleaver over her head. "I told you to go away."

When the shadow stayed on the wall, the mother struck at the shadow's head and stepped back. To her horror, the head vanished, but the rest of the shadow remained. She struck at the body and the body disappeared. "Go away, go away." Frantically she chopped at the shadow's arms and legs until only the hands and feet were left.

The mother stood panting. Then one hand began to dance like a spider and then the other. The next moment both feet began to leap and hop about. When the head reappeared, the feet began to kick it about like a ball. Finally, the arms, legs, and body appeared. They bounced all about the house.

The mother realized that the ghost was only playing with her. The only damage she had done was to her walls. And in the morning, her daughter could not move her arms.

The girl lay stiff and helpless in bed. The tears ran down her cheeks, and she could not even wipe them away. "Don't let him take me."

The mother gently wiped the tears away. "Of course not."

The girl rolled her eyes so she could stare at her mother. "How are you going to stop him?"

The mother bit her lip helplessly. "I don't know."

The tears began rolling from the frightened girl's eyes again. "I don't want to marry a ghost."

That gave the determined mother another idea, so she told her daughter to stop. "He wants a bride, but perhaps it doesn't matter who it is."

She went back to the wise old woman, and the old woman suggested a woman who had also died young. Together, they got the consent of her parents and then hurriedly prepared a wedding.

They did everything as if both people had been alive. A

red sedan chair was carried to the house of the mother of the dead girl. There, the mother of the sick girl put food and bridal clothes of paper in the chair. Then some young men carried the chair out of the village.

When they first set out, the chair had been light because it only carried food and some paper cutouts. But gradually it grew heavier and heavier until the chair sagged between the poles. The young men had to move slower and said it felt as if they were carrying a real person.

At the stone, the people acted as they would at a real marriage feast. The women even brought hot water and poured it into a basin so the ghost groom could wash his face. When the wedding was over and they were cleaning up, they found the water inside the basin was dirty.

"He must be pleased," the wise old woman said. "He's washed his face like a real person."

When the mother finally returned home, she found her daughter standing in the doorway to greet her.

The Butterfly Man

ONE SUMMER THE PLANTS WILTED in the fields. No matter what the farmers tried to do, the rice stalks bent over in the fields like so many old people. The farmers tried every cure and every prayer, but nothing helped.

Finally, one farmer gave up. He threw down his hoe and went to his older brother. "There's no luck here this year. Let's find work elsewhere."

"I've always wanted to see something of the world," said the older brother. "But don't be in such a hurry to throw your hoe away. We'll need it next year." So the practical brother picked up his brother's hoe and brought both their tools to his house.

Then the two brothers went to a faraway city and found work. "We've never been this far away from home," the older brother said. "We should make the most of it."

The younger brother grinned. "And I was just starting to lose hope for you, brother." He started to turn to the right while his older brother turned to the left. "Where are you going? The wine shops are this way."

The older brother took hold of his younger brother and tried to pull him along. "But the marketplace is this way. There are all sorts of folks who lecture for free."

But the younger brother was a head taller and twenty kilos heavier than his older brother. "I'm going to have fun for the first time in my life, and you can't stop me."

The older brother argued for a while longer, but he knew he was helpless. At home, there were family and friends to help him hold back his little brother. But in this strange place, he was the only one and he wasn't enough, so he had to let his little brother go his own way.

Although the two brothers didn't earn very much, the younger brother spent most of his earnings on wine and gambling. But his older brother sent home some extra money for both their families.

At the end of the year they started back for their village. In his basket the older brother had candies for his children and a piece of red silk ribbon for his wife; in his head he had hundreds of sights and scenes to describe to the rest of the clan. The younger brother only had enough money for a jar of tiger whiskey.

On the way home, the two brothers had to pass through tall, wooded mountains. Near a village, children were swarming around an old beggar like ants around a crippled beetle.

His dirty, matted hair hung down like a black tattered curtain to his shoulders, and his robes were ragged and filled with holes. The monk only had one sandal; and he smelled as if he had not had a bath in months.

"Go away!" one boy shrieked gleefully. "We don't want beggars here." He hit the beggar with a stick.

A girl had an even longer stick of bamboo with which she prodded and poked the beggar.

The beggar didn't know which way to turn. No sooner did he face one tormentor then another one struck him. He was an old man bent almost double and with feet callused and gnarled as a tree's roots. The old man's ribs showed through the torn shirt and his skin was covered with sores. He leaned on a crutch and gourd bumped against his hip every time he turned. But he did not try to strike the children. He merely shook a long, withered stalk of grass.

"Stop that!" the older brother said to the children. "Can't you see he's a fool?"

But a boy only threw a rock at him. "Mind your own business."

There were men and women at the gates. They were laughing as if this were a puppet show. "It all comes back," the older brother warned them, "if not in this life than in another."

A man leaned lazily against the gatepost. "We're tired of beggars coming through here, so we let the children play a little."

The older brother shook his head. "A fine thing for them to learn."

The man spat. "Dragons take care of dragons. Tigers take care of tigers."

The younger brother touched his brother's arm. "He's

right. In times of need, each clan has to take care of its own and not strangers."

But right then, the old beggar set the grass blade between his teeth, stooped, and picked up a handful of dirt. And there was something about the beggar's eyes that made the older brother stop. Even as he watched, the beggar threw the dust up and the wind scattered it away.

The older brother was not the simple man he had been when he had first gone to the city. He had heard of holy fools who spoke with inspired wisdom, whose sermons came directly from their souls. Sometimes they spouted what sounded like nonsense or did silly gestures. But the wise understood the real meaning.

The older brother stopped his brother. "Don't you see what he's saying? We are all one. We come from the dust and we go back to it."

"He's just crazy," the younger brother insisted.

But the older brother demanded, "Are you a master?"

"Once I was a butterfly," the beggar murmured. "I dreamed I was a man who dreamed he was a butterfly. Now I'm never sure."

"Are you a master?" the farmer repeated again.

The beggar began to bellow like a water buffalo.

"You see?" his younger brother asked in disgust.

But holy or not, the beggar moved the older farmer to pity. "That could be me someday," he thought. He opened up his basket and took out a handful of candy.

"That's for your children," his younger brother protested.

"The beggar needs it more." He tossed the candy in the air. "Here. Treats."

The children instantly scrambled about in the dirt, fighting for the candy.

Taking the beggar by the arm, the older brother led him away from the heartless village. They walked higher into the mountains until they came to a crossroads. Here, the beggar started to take the lower road. . . But the two farmers had to go higher past the ruins of an old castle.

"We part company here," the older farmer said. "I hope your path is smoother from now on."

But the beggar hobbled around so he could stare at the two brothers. "Jealousy sleeps but never dies. The hand will take long after flesh and bone are dust."

The younger brother laughed. "More nonsense."

"The sword rusts. The spear breaks." The beggar held out the blade of grass. "But this endures. You know it. They know it."

The older brother was reluctant to take the blade of grass after the beggar had sucked on it. "Who's they?"

The beggar jerked his head up toward the stone ruins. "A general of old rose up against the emperor of the north. Mighty was his army. Splendid was his court. But he is gone and we remain."

"It takes more than ghost stories to scare me," the younger brother said. "Or to get a donation out of me."

The beggar urged the older brother to take the grass. "Keep this on your tongue to keep it wet. Then you'll be safe. Don't and you won't."

When the older brother took the blade of grass, the younger brother made fun of him. "I didn't think you were superstitious."

"Call it a souvenir." The farmer tucked the blade of grass behind his ear.

"Come on. He's held us up long enough." The younger brother set off on the road and the older brother followed.

When the older brother looked back, he could not see the old man. "He's gone."

His brother snorted. "Some bend in the road must have hidden him."

Toward sunset, they came to a broad terrace. Grass grew between the cracks in the stones, but they could still make out the fine carving.

"I can't say much for the housekeeping," the younger brother said, "but the view is magnificent."

In the distance, the mountains rose, their shoulders dusted with green shrubbery and their heads crowned with white clouds.

"If it's fit for a king, it's fit for us," the older brother agreed.

The two brothers sat down on the ruined terrace. There they made a meal of rice. The younger brother tried to share his tiger whiskey with his older brother, but the older brother refused.

"I'll stick with water," the older farmer said. "I want a clear head tonight."

"Now you're letting an old beggar talk you out of a good time." The younger brother drank from the jar until the whiskey was all gone.

Although they were lying on hard stone, the younger brother was so drunk that he soon fell asleep. But the older brother stayed wide awake.

For a brief moment, a blue light flickered through the

old stones. The older farmer reached for his brother. "Wake up."

But the light was gone by the time the brother opened his eyes and raised his head. "What?"

"It's gone now."

"That old monk's spooked you." The younger brother lay back down again.

But the older brother took the grass from behind his ear and broke off a bit. "Maybe we'd better suck on this."

The younger brother looked disgusted. "Not after the grass has been in his mouth."

But the older brother put the piece of grass in his mouth anyway. Suddenly the blue light rose from behind a statue, casting strange shadows across the terrace. It darted to the left and to the right like a hunting hound trying to catch a scent.

The older brother turned to his brother when the blue light suddenly flashed over them. For a moment, he could see nothing in the blinding light, but he could smell the scent of dust and old incense; and then the blue light flashed away.

He blinked his eyes for several moments. "Did you see that?" he asked.

His brother groped blindly for him. "Give me some of the beggar's plant."

The older brother handed the rest to his little brother. By the time he regained his eyesight, a greenish glow had filled the tangled bushes of the hill. It spread outward like a pool across the terrace, and within the greenish light he could see ghosts in antique robes and armor. They moved slowly as unseen musicians played a sad, weary tune. And he could hear their voices—high and thin and scratchy like old leaves caught in a breeze and skittering across stones.

And as they passed, the brothers could see that some had no eyes. Others had tongues that floated in front of their open mouths. Still others had eyeballs that rolled around within the eye sockets. Finally came one ghost in costly armor and with a crown. He turned to stare angrily at the two brothers; as he looked at them, his eyes melted and poured down his face like milk.

He followed the other ghosts around the broad terrace and vanished back among the tangled bushes. "So the beggar wasn't such a fool after all," the older brother said.

But there was no answer. He turned to look for his brother, but his brother was gone. Then he realized that his brother's mouth had gone dry with fear. He called for his brother, but the light only faded from the hill and the music vanished in the distance.

Virtues and Vices

A culture defines its virtues and vices within its folk tales. Kindness sometimes brings rewards in this life, as the lonely old woman discovers with her superior pet mouse in "The Superior Pet."

Kindness to animals would affirm Buddhist beliefs. Moreover, tales such as "We Are All One" would have had special poignancy for the old-timers. Many came from small villages in China that were occupied by one clan, which provided an elaborate support network. In America, they had to set up their own, organizing by district, family, and so on. Even for later arrivals, the sense of unity would have been necessary in the urban ghettos of later times.

Again, any of the new immigrants to America might have felt lost in this strange new country—just as the young man did in the marshlands in "Snake-Spoke."

Defining vices is as important as defining virtues. Greed is universally denounced, but also implicit is the message that one must be moderate in desires. In a culture that demanded sacrifice and hard work, the message was a necessary one. They would have understood the argumentative yet humble old woman in "The Old Jar."

Old-timers would have understood, too, the moral of "The Boasting Contest." There was already a Chinese proverb to the effect that the nail that stuck out the most got hammered. Immigrants striving to survive in America, where visibility often brought persecution, would have stressed that idea. Under such conditions, bragging was more than foolish; it was suicidal. Equally destructive was jealousy. Where there were so many people and so little land, water, and resources, cooperation was necessary.

We
Are
All
One

LONG AGO THERE WAS A RICH MAN with a disease in his eyes. For many years, the pain was so great that he could not sleep at night. He saw every doctor he could, but none of them could help him.

"What good is all my money?" he groaned. Finally, he became so desperate that he sent criers through the city offering a reward to anyone who could cure him.

Now in that city lived an old candy peddler. He would walk around with his baskets of candy, but he was so kind-hearted that he gave away as much as he sold, so he was always poor.

When the old peddler heard the announcement, he remembered something his mother had said. She had once told him about a magical herb that was good for the eyes. So he packed up his baskets and went back to the single tiny room in which his family lived.

When he told his plan to his wife, she scolded him, "If

73

you go off on this crazy hunt, how are we supposed to eat?"

Usually the peddler gave in to his wife, but this time he was stubborn. "There are two baskets of candy," he said. "I'll be back before they're gone."

The next morning, as soon as the soldiers opened the gates, he was the first one to leave the city. He did not stop until he was deep inside the woods. As a boy, he had often wandered there. He had liked to pretend that the shadowy forest was a green sea and he was a fish slipping through the cool waters.

As he examined the ground, he noticed ants scurrying about. On their backs were larvae like white grains of rice. A rock had fallen into a stream, so the water now spilled into the ant's nest.

"We're all one," the kind-hearted peddler said. So he waded into the shallow stream and put the rock on the bank. Then with a sharp stick, he dug a shallow ditch that sent the rest of the water back into the stream.

Without another thought about his good deed, he began to search through the forest. He looked everywhere; but as the day went on, he grew sleepy. "Ho-hum. I got up too early. I'll take just a short nap," he decided, and lay down in the shade of an old tree, where he fell right asleep.

In his dreams, the old peddler found himself standing in the middle of a great city. Tall buildings rose high overhead. He couldn't see the sky even when he tilted back his head. An escort of soldiers marched up to him with a loud clatter of their black lacquer armor. "Our queen wishes to see you," the captain said.

The frightened peddler could only obey and let the fierce soldiers lead him into a shining palace. There, a woman with a high crown sat upon a tall throne. Trembling, the old peddler fell to his knees and touched his forehead against the floor.

But the queen ordered him to stand. "Like the great Emperor Yü of long ago, you tamed the great flood. We are all one now. You have only to ask, and I or any of my people will come to your aid."

The old peddler cleared his throat. "I am looking for a certain herb. It will cure any disease of the eyes."

The queen shook her head regretfully. "I have never heard of that herb. But you will surely find it if you keep looking for it."

And then the old peddler woke. Sitting up, he saw that in his wanderings he had come back to the ants' nest. It was there he had taken his nap. His dream city had been the ant's nest itself.

"This is a good omen," he said to himself, and he began searching even harder. He was so determined to find the herb that he did not notice how time had passed. He was surprised when he saw how the light was fading. He looked all around then. There was no sight of his city—only strange hills. He realized then that he had searched so far he had gotten lost.

Night was coming fast and with it the cold. He rubbed his arms and hunted for shelter. In the twilight, he thought he could see the green tiles of a roof.

He stumbled through the growing darkness until he reached a ruined temple. Weeds grew through cracks in the stones and most of the roof itself had fallen in. Still, the ruins would provide some protection.

As he started inside, he saw a centipede with bright

orange skin and red tufts of fur along its back. Yellow dots covered its sides like a dozen tiny eyes. It was also rushing into the temple as fast as it could, but there was a bird swooping down toward it.

The old peddler waved his arms and shouted, scaring the bird away. Then he put down his palm in front of the insect. "We are all one, you and I." The many feet tickled his skin as the centipede climbed onto his hand.

Inside the temple, he gathered dried leaves and found old sticks of wood and soon he had a fire going. The peddler even picked some fresh leaves for the centipede from a bush near the temple doorway. "I may have to go hungry, but you don't have to, friend."

Stretching out beside the fire, the old peddler pillowed his head on his arms. He was so tired that he soon fell asleep, but even in his sleep he dreamed he was still search-ing in the woods. Suddenly he thought he heard footsteps near his head. He woke instantly and looked about, but he only saw the brightly colored centipede.

"Was it you, friend?" The old peddler chuckled and, lying down, he closed his eyes again. "I must be getting nervous."

"We are one, you and I," a voice said faintly—as if from a long distance. "If you go south, you will find a pine tree with two trunks. By its roots, you will find a magic bead. A cousin of mine spat on it years ago. Dissolve that bead in wine and tell the rich man to drink it if he wants to heal his eyes."

The old peddler trembled when he heard the voice, be-cause he realized that the centipede was magical. He wanted to run from the temple, but he couldn't even get up. It was as if he were glued to the floor.

But then the old peddler reasoned with himself: If the centipede had wanted to hurt me, it could have long ago. Instead, it seems to want to help me.

So the old peddler stayed where he was, but he did not dare open his eyes. When the first sunlight fell through the roof, he raised one eyelid cautiously. There was no sign of the centipede. He sat up and looked around, but the magical centipede was gone.

He followed the centipede's instructions when he left the temple. Traveling south, he kept a sharp eye out for the pine tree with two trunks. He walked until late in the afternoon, but all he saw were normal pine trees.

Wearily he sat down and sighed. Even if he found the pine tree, he couldn't be sure that he would find the bead. Someone else might even have discovered it a long time ago.

But something made him look a little longer. Just when he was thinking about turning back, he saw the odd tree. Somehow his tired legs managed to carry him over to the tree, and he got down on his knees. But the ground was covered with pine needles and his old eyes were too weak. The old peddler could have wept with frustration, and then he remembered the ants.

He began to call, "Ants, ants, we are all one."

Almost immediately, thousands of ants came boiling out of nowhere. Delighted, the old man held up his fingers. "I'm looking for a bead. It might be very tiny."

Then, careful not to crush any of his little helpers, the

old man sat down to wait. In no time, the ants reappeared with a tiny bead. With trembling fingers, the old man took the bead from them and examined it. It was colored orange and looked as if it had yellow eyes on the sides.

There was nothing very special about the bead, but the old peddler treated it like a fine jewel. Putting the bead into his pouch, the old peddler bowed his head. "I thank you and I thank your queen," the old man said. After the ants disappeared among the pine needles, he made his way out of the woods.

The next day, he reached the house of the rich man. However, he was so poor and ragged that the gatekeeper only laughed at him. "How could an old beggar like you help my master?"

The old peddler tried to argue. "Beggar or rich man, we are all one."

But it so happened that the rich man was passing by the gates. He went over to the old peddler. "I said anyone could see me. But it'll mean a stick across your back if you're wasting my time."

The old peddler took out the pouch. "Dissolve this bead in some wine and drink it down." Then, turning the pouch upside down, he shook the tiny bead onto his palm and handed it to the rich man.

The rich man immediately called for a cup of wine. Dropping the bead into the wine, he waited a moment and then drank it down. Instantly the pain vanished. Shortly after that, his eyes healed.

The rich man was so happy and grateful that he doubled the reward. And the kindly old peddler and his family lived comfortably for the rest of their lives.

The
Superior
Pet

ONCE THERE WAS A FAMILY that lost all its money. They had to sell their big house and all their fields, but the parents could not forget they had once been rich, and they did not let their daughter forget either.

Out of all their vast wealth, they managed to keep only a silver ear scoop. It was a slender silver spoon about five inches long. People put it into their ears to take out the wax.

"It's a silly enough thing," her father used to say, "but from it we'll rebuild the family fortune somehow."

When the daughter grew old enough to marry, no rich family wanted her with only an ear scoop for a dowry, and her parents thought poor farmers were beneath her.

When her parents died, no one wanted her. She lived with other unmarried women in a house that the clan provided, but it was very crowded. She lived there many years.

Although she sewed from sunrise to sunset, she was still very poor. As she got older, her eyes got worse. Soon, she could not sew the fine stitches she once had. As a result, even though she worked just as hard as before, she got less money. Eventually, she could no longer pay her share of the food and other costs.

"Why don't you sell that old ear scoop?" the other women would ask her.

"It's all I have from my parents," the old woman said indignantly.

Because she had been in the house so long, she had a nice spot in a corner, but the other women wanted her to move to another place.

"You can't pay your share and yet you take up all that space," the other women complained. They found dozens of little ways to be unpleasant. Among other things, she always had to be last—even to use the wash water. They would give her only the stringiest vegetables and the weakest tea. And they always served her rice scraped from the bottom, which was hard and crunchy and difficult for the old woman's teeth to chew.

One day, a younger cousin caught a mouse. But in catching it, she had injured one of its feet. "Look at this thing. It's all white."

"That proves it must be a superior mouse," the old woman said. "There's not another like it in the district."

"The pest is probably a superior eater too," her cousin said. "I'm not going to have it nibbling at our food and clothes."

But the mouse looked so small and fragile and helpless that the old woman knew it needed her. She had never had anyone to love, and, as such things go, her heart fixed on the mouse. A superior mouse will make a superior pet, she thought to herself. And out loud she said, "Give it to me. I'll get rid of it."

Her cousin was glad to give the unpleasant task to the old woman. "Here then."

But the old woman did not kill the mouse. Instead, she kept it in a little box. She made a soft nest for it out of scraps of cloth. She even went hungry so she could save some of her rice for her superior pet. In time, the mouse's foot healed.

One day, though, her cousin found the mouse. "You old liar. You kept that filthy little thing."

She was going to throw the box down the well, but the old woman grabbed it from her. "This is mine. It's a superior mouse."

"You've gone too far this time. Beggars can't act like empresses," her cousin said. She called all the other women around her. Naturally, they took the cousin's side.

The old woman clutched the box to her and looked at the circle of hard, stern faces. She saw no mercy there. "I'll go," she said in a small voice.

Her cousin was surprised. "You've never been away from the village in your life."

"Then I'll learn." The old woman packed her few belongings quickly—including the ear scoop. Then she left the house where she had lived all those years. I should be afraid, she thought to herself, but I feel years younger. She gave a little skip as she walked away from her village and up into the hills.

She looked for roots and plants for herself and her mouse. But it was autumn, and the villagers had already stripped the hills bare looking for fuel.

It was cold that night, and the old woman kept the box against her stomach to keep her pet warm. The next day she wandered even farther. But she still found nothing to eat.

Finally, she came to a wall that paralleled the road. Beyond the wall lay only a few old moss-covered stones and bushes.

Her feet ached with the cold and exertion, so she sat down with her back against the wall. On her lap she set out the box with her superior mouse. Then she opened the lid so it could breathe. Then she took out the silver ear scoop and held it in front of her pet. "We'll have to sell this. But the money won't last forever. And then what will we do?"

But the ear scoop dropped from her nervous fingers and fell into the weeds.

"Now I'll have to clean it." As she bent to get it, the white mouse leaped from her lap and onto the ground. Snatching up the spoon between its teeth, the mouse scurried to the wall. Desperately the old woman tried to grab the mouse, but it vanished through a crack in the wall.

"You ungrateful little thief," the old woman said. "I gave up everything for you. Is this how you repay me?" Anger made her forget that she was cold and tired.

She dug and tore at the crumbling old bricks, and when her fingers began to bleed, she picked up a sharp stick instead and began to pry them out. She pulled brick after brick away from the wall, and still there was no sign of the furry bandit.

When she lifted the final brick from the spot, the last of the sunlight winked off something. Hardly daring to breathe, she dug into the dirt itself. There, buried in the earth was a large golden vase. She scrabbled even deeper and found more objects of gold and silver. And beneath them was a pile of emeralds and rubies and pearls. And right in the middle of the pile of jewels was her silver ear scoop.

The superior mouse had repaid her kindness before it had gone on its way. And in certain parts of China, the farm folk still think that white mice bring good luck.

Snake-
Spoke

ONCE THERE WAS A YOUNG MAN with very little patience. When his family fell on hard times, his father told him to ask a friend to repay a loan.

Before he let his son leave, the father took a charm from around his neck and tied it around his son's neck. "This has the name of the Protector written on it. The priest who sold it to me said it would chase any demon away. Even so, just remember: hasty head, hasty feet, hasty end."

The young man thought he knew everything. "I only seem impatient because you do things so slow. Times are changing and we have to change with them."

He left his home in the hills and traveled down toward the city. Because the villagers in the flatlands lived closer to the city, their tools and houses, hair and clothes, everything was more up-to-date. But as hard as he looked, the young man did not see any charms around anyone else's neck.

"If people see this, they'll think I'm a hick." So he tucked the charm inside his shirt.

Even though the road passed through the marsh, there was a good deal of traffic in the daytime. As the road had left the marshlands, a sedan chair trotted past him. He thought he heard a girl giggle from inside the chair. The young traveler stopped and his face blushed a bright red.

"She must have seen the cord to this stupid charm and known what I was wearing. This is fine for a superstitious old man like father but not for a modern young man like me." So he tore the charm from his neck and threw it away.

Feeling more sophisticated, he almost strutted into the great city. He went to the address his father had given him; but the people there sent him to the dockside. He was asking all around the docks when a sweaty worker suddenly called to him. It was his father's friend.

The son tried not to stare at the man's dirty, ragged clothes as he explained his mission.

The friend sadly hit his head. "I'm sorry. If I could pay you, I would. Once I had three ships filled with spices. But I've lost everything. Now I unload ships to earn my food."

The young man said, "My father was counting on you."

But the friend spread out his hands. "You don't find wine in an empty cup."

Disgusted, the young man wheeled around without another word and left the docks. "If father had let me invest the money, we'd still be rich. Instead, he had to give it to that fool." He was in such a hurry to tell his father "I told you so" that he started right back for home.

By late afternoon, the young man had once again reached the edge of the marshes. There, sitting by a rock, was a big, fierce man with the strangest black cap. Its sides were spread out like a bat's wings.

The man in the cap glared at the young man. "You'd do better to wait till the morning before you go into the marsh."

The young man put on a superior expression. "How do you expect to get anywhere if you just laze the day away on a rock?" And he marched straight past the man in the cap and down the road into the marshlands.

"Then at least don't talk to strangers," the man in the cap called after him.

The young man just laughed. "You don't even keep your own advice." And the man's warning went right out of his mind.

By sunset he was almost at the other end of the marsh, but a thick mist began to rise. Soon he couldn't see the road at all. He began to shuffle along, but the mist became so thick that he couldn't even see his feet. He had to get down on all fours and crawl along like a dog with his head bent to see the road. Centimeter by centimeter, he made his way through the mist.

Suddenly, he heard someone call to him from the mist. "Where are you going, s-s-stranger? Have you eaten ri-c-ce?"

The young man was so relieved that he spoke up right away. "I'm lost and haven't eaten all day. Could you direct me to an inn?"

The mist thinned out enough for him to see the silhouette of a man's head. "Yes-s-s, I could, Mis-s-s-ter—?"

The young man got up off the ground and began to walk toward the man. "It's Siu. And you're Mister—?"

"Mis-s-s-ter Ssiu, Mis-s-s-ter Ss-s-iu, Mis-s-s-ter Ss-s-iu," the stranger repeated gleefully.

"What's wrong? Don't go without me." The young man ran recklessly toward the stranger, but when he got closer, he saw that the head rested on a thick column that swayed like a tree in a strong wind. The young man stopped. "Who are you? What are you?" he demanded.

"Mis-s-s-ter Ss-s-iu, Mis-s-s-ter Ss-s-iu, Mis-s-s-ter Ss-s-iu," the stranger hissed and vanished.

As the young man shuffled forward carefully, he felt the mist but there was nothing. "It must have been some trick of the mist that made his body look so funny. But where did he go?"

Luckily for the young man, the mist itself began to rise above the ground. In the distance, he could make out the lanterns of an inn twinkling like friendly little stars.

Grateful, he headed straight for them. But when he pounded on the gates, the innkeeper stared at him over the gates. "Did anyone call your name just now?"

"Yes," the young man said. "Is he here already?"

The innkeeper sighed and shook his head sadly. "Sorry. You're snake-spoke."

"But I can pay." The astonished young man began to dig for his money.

The innkeeper nodded toward the misty road. "When you're snake-spoke, you're snake meat. There's a monster in the marsh. You could be the richest person in the world but your wealth wouldn't save you when he's got your name."

Suddenly one of the guests stepped out of the inn. It was the man with the cap. "Let our hasty young friend in. He's a fool, but his father would miss him."

The innkeeper got down and stared at the man in the funny cap. "Don't order me around in my own inn."

There was a tame parrot sleeping on a perch. The man in the cap went over to it. "You should be more worried about the evil inside your inn rather than what's outside."

When the man grabbed the bird's legs, it rose with a startled squawk.

"You're crazy. Let the bird go," the innkeeper ordered.

But the man in the cap merely smiled. "All nature is an open book to me. Shall I real the bird's face?"

The bird had turned and snapped at the man's wrist with its great beak. But the man seized the beak and held it shut. He stretched a finger down to touch a certain spot upon the bird's neck. Instantly, its eyes began to glow a bright yellow and flicker like flames.

The man in the cap risked letting go of the beak and reached a hand into one of his large sleeves. The bird's head darted forward to snap at him, but he had his charm out already—a sword made from strings of coins.

Instantly the bird began to blur. Its bright feathers became spots of color that began to whirl around and around; as the colors spun, they began to darken until they were almost black.

"What did I ever do to you?" demanded the little dark whirlwind.

"I was sent to rid the world of evil." The man in the cap

flung the whirlwind into the air and it spun up into the night sky.

The awed innkeeper drew the bar back from the gates and let the now frightened traveler into the courtyard. When he saw his savior, the young man bowed his head. "I take back my hasty words to you."

"That's a start." The man in the cap pulled a small section of bamboo out of his robe. The cylinder was about as long as his finger and just as thick. It was sealed at both ends by thick pieces of oiled paper. "Put this under your head tonight, but whatever you do, don't go to sleep."

"And where will you be?" the young man asked.

"I'll be trying to catch the snake," the man in the cap said. "But snakes are tricky. If I miss him and he gets into the room, this bamboo will begin to shake and rattle. Open it up quickly. But don't you dare open it if the snake isn't around."

The young man took the bamboo and examined it. "What's inside?"

"Let's hope you never have to find out." The man in the cap nodded to the innkeeper, and the innkeeper led the traveler inside to a room.

There were several other people sharing the broad boards of the bed. "Not another guest. There's no more room," one of them grumbled.

"He's snake-spoke," the innkeeper said.

People immediately rolled off the bed and scurried out of the room to find someplace else in the inn—preferably far away from the doomed man.

The young man put the bamboo down on the bed and then he put his sack of belongings down on top of that.

While he was trying to get comfortable, the innkeeper left. He bustled back a moment later with boards, nails, and a hammer.

"Maybe this will help." The innkeeper quickly hammered some boards over the window. Wishing the young man good luck, the innkeeper left with his lantern.

The room was pitch black, but the young man groped about blindly until he found a chair and wedged that against the door.

I'll hear the snake if he tries to break in now, the man thought. He groped his way back to the bed and lay down with his head on his sack.

As soon as he heard the rattling sound, his hand shot behind his head for the bamboo. But the cylinder was quiet against his palm.

It must have been a wind at the window, he told himself. Impatience got me into this mess. Patience will have to get me out of it. For once, I'm going to do what I'm told. Nervously he lay back down again as he repeated his father's warning. "Hasty head, hasty feet, hasty end."

Every creak and groan of that old inn made the man reach for the bamboo, but each time he realized it was a false alarm. However, after several hours, the man became so exhausted that he fell asleep.

No one saw the man in the cap reach the roof in one great leap. He sat down there to watch and wait for the snake. But the snake was as cunning as it was old. It changed itself into a worm hardly bigger than a fingernail and inched its way under the barred gate. It was so tiny that the man in the cap did not see it as it crept across the courtyard.

No one heard it as it slipped under the locked door of the inn. It knew where the young man was. It could smell him. It could smell his fear. It crawled underneath the door of the room and looked around. It could see as well in the dark as it could during the day. It laughed when it saw the chair and the boarded window.

The man lay snoring fretfully on the bed. With a magic word, the snake changed itself back to its true form. Slowly, it slithered across the floor toward the bed.

Suddenly the bamboo beneath the young man began to shake and quiver, and there was a loud rattling sound like dozens of tiny drums beating crazily.

He opened his eyes but it was so dark in the room that he could see nothing. But he could hear the sound of leather scraping stone and realized that must be the monster wriggling toward him.

He grabbed the bamboo from underneath the sack. It was shaking so much that it almost jumped out of his hand. Quickly he thrust two fingers through the paper. There was an angry buzzing and dozens of flying ants tickled his fingers as they flew past. They darted right into the monster's nostrils and began to bite at its insides.

The snake gave a high, thin hiss like a kettle bouncing on a hot fire. It threw itself headfirst at the window. The boards and shutters shattered into splinters, and the man could see its long, scaly body sliding through the window.

"Got you!" the man in the cap shouted, and jumped down from the roof right onto the snake's back.

The young man ran to the window and watched the man in the cap battle the giant snake. Sometimes the man in the cap was completely hidden by its great coils, but one hand or a foot or his head would always appear and the man in the cap would throw off the snake. They battled all around the courtyard, smashing a cart, barrels, and boxes.

And in the end, the man in the cap killed the snake and caught its evil soul within a gourd. "You're safe now," he told the young man as he stoppered the gourd.

The innkeeper ran outside and pointed at his courtyard. "I trusted you and you've wrecked my place."

"Let this young man pay for it as a fee for his lesson." The man in the cap picked up the snake and broke it in half over his knee. "Next time," he said to the young man, "don't be afraid to be a hick. What people think of you isn't the important thing. It's what you are yourself." And with a kick of his heels, he rose into the sky and disappeared.

Instantly, the young man knelt and bowed. He realized that the man in the cap could only be the Protector.

In the meantime, the innkeeper wagged his finger at the young man. "You're going to work off all the damages."

But the young man looked at the exposed joints of the snake. Within the bone was a small ball with a rainbow sheen. In each joint was a pearl, and there were as many joints as in a bamboo stem. The pearls were more than enough to pay for the repairs to the inn and to restore the family's fortunes.

He paid the innkeeper for the damages and returned home a more patient—and richer—person.

The
Old
Jar

ALL HER LIFE A CERTAIN WOMAN never did what anyone wanted. She never asked for charity, but she wouldn't be cheated out of what was hers either. However, she finally grew too old to work in the fields. She sold her furniture piece by piece until all she had was a pot and one jar full of rice. Although she ate only one meal a day, the rice slowly dwindled until she was down to her last two bowlfuls.

Then she broke the jar. She went to the corner and dug in the dirt and took out her savings. All she had was three cash—round coins with holes in the center.

"I was going to buy rice with this, but now I couldn't keep the mice out of the rice. I'll have to buy a new jar," she decided.

So she gathered up the rice from the floor. Carefully she

went through the broken pieces of the jar until she had picked up every grain. Then she poured all the rice into a small pouch and put the three coins on top. Satisfied, she closed up the pouch and put it into her sleeve.

Leaving her little house, she took the road into town. She had never been to town before, so the two-story houses looked like mansions to her, and the mansions looked like the palaces of an emperor. From the restaurants came the most delicious aromas: dumplings and duck and a dozen other delicacies. The old woman was so hungry that she almost went in and bought something. But then she bit her lip. "Rice has always been good enough for you before this. It will be good enough now."

She marched straight into a shop that was crammed with every kind of good thing to buy—statues, vases, and all kinds of knickknacks.

A clerk threaded his way through the narrow aisles. He was dressed in a silk robe and a black vest and on his head was a black cap. "What do you want, you old beggar? This isn't a museum." He got ready to throw her out of the store.

The old woman took the pouch from her sleeve and shook it so that her three coins jingled. When the clerk heard the sound and saw how full the pouch was, he thought she was rich.

Instantly he was all smiles and bows. "Why does a rich woman like madam dress like a beggar? Let me show you some silks."

"Silk indeed!" the old woman snorted. "Cotton keeps out the sun and cold just as well."

"Now I know how madam got rich," the clerk sighed. "Well, how can I serve you?"

The old woman folded her hands in front of her. "I need a jar."

"We have some antique jars that go back to the Ming dynasty." The clerk led her over to some bright-blue vases around which dragons curled. "The clay came from the bed of a pure mountain stream, and the potter made only one vase a year."

The old woman pretended to look and shook her head. "That's a bit fancy for what I had in mind."

"Well, we have some excellent celadon vases done in the classic style of the Sung dynasty." The clerk led her over to some green vases.

The old woman tapped a vase with her fingernail. "Not very sturdy."

The clerk showed her almost every vase in the shop, but each time the old woman found something wrong with it. Finally, they wound up in the dim rear of the store. "Madam," the clerk said, "you've seen every vase in the store."

The old woman saw a large, plain earthenware jar on the floor. It was only as high as her knee, but it was solidly made. "What's that?"

The clerk picked up the heavy reddish-brown jar in both arms and dusted off the dirt. "This? It's cracked at the top. We just use it to catch water from the leak in the roof. But it doesn't even do a good job of that. Water pours out of it like it's a well."

The old woman thought to herself, Crack or not, it would

still keep out the mice. "It reminds me of something my grandmother had. How much?"

"A hundred cash," the clerk said.

The old woman glared up at the clerk. "Sentiment goes only so far. You just said it had a crack and—"

The clerk thrust the jar at the old woman. "Ten cash then."

However, the old woman did not take the jar. "Humph," she sniffed. "You're awful eager to get rid of it. Why should I take your garbage? It's a big jar and the road home is a long one."

"You've wasted enough of my time," the clerk snapped. "Just take it then. And good riddance to the jar and you."

The old woman laughed to herself, these townfolk don't know how to bargain. But out loud, she asked, "Aren't you going to pay me to take it off your hands?"

"I never met a more contrary person in this whole city than you. Out, out, out!" the clerk shouted angrily.

Still chuckling to herself, the old woman set the jar on her head. Then she walked carefully down the narrow aisles because she didn't want to break one of the expensive antiques. She left the city. However, at each step the jar felt heavier and heavier, so she stopped by a farmer's house.

"You're a heavy thing," she said to the old jar. "You must have sides as thick as the city wall."

The farmer's wife was working in the garden. When she saw the jar, she called out to the road. "Hey, Auntie, that jar would be perfect for my garden. I'll just turn it upside down and use it as a stool."

"It's a jar for rice," the old woman panted, "not for people's bottoms."

"But what do you need with that heavy, broken old thing?" the wife asked. "I'll trade you a good jar, and it'll be small enough to carry."

The old woman wiped the sweat from her eyes. She was tempted, but then she thought to herself, It's old and un-wanted—just like me. So out loud she said, "It deserves to end its days inside a nice house instead of outside in the mud. Get some pretty pink porcelain stools."

"Humph," the farmer's wife huffed, "you beat the whole district for contrariness."

"That I do," the old woman agreed.

Tipping the jar over on its round side, she began to roll the jar along. But even so, the jar began to grow as heavy. She felt as if she were trying to move a boulder. She began a soft little work chant, "Mice from the rice, mice from the rice, mice from the rice."

Halfway to the village, a cart driver came up behind her. "Is that a jar or a melon, Auntie?"

The old woman looked behind her and went on shoving the jar. "I'm not your auntie—thank Heaven. And this is a jar."

The cart driver slowed down when he reached her. "That's just the thing to break up for paving tiles. I'll give you a hundred cash for it."

The old woman was tempted. The jar kept growing heav-ier, and the road home was a long one. With the money she could buy not only a smaller jar but rice as well. But then she looked down at the big, cracked jar.

"It's outlived its usefulness—just like me. So I think I'll keep it." And she kept rolling the jar along.

"If they had a contrary contest, you'd take first place in

a whole province of contrary people," the driver said, and passed her on the road.

At least I'm improving, the old woman thought to herself and she began to shove her jar along. "Mice from the rice, mice from the rice."

As she neared the village, the jar seemed to become bigger and heavier with every step she took. To take her mind off the effort, she began to talk to the jar. "What put the crack in your top?" she puffed. "Where have you been and what's been done to you? Have you carried oils to India? Have you traveled into the desert in an army wagon? You served everybody faithfully, and when they were finished with you, they just threw you away until you wound up in that shop."

And as she struggled along, she kept thinking about the jar until it almost seemed like a friend. She went on pushing the jar until she reached her village. However, the road now wound back and forth up the steep side of the valley. And as she tried to shove the jar along the road, she found herself slipping. For every two steps she took, she slid back one.

The other villagers left the fields and the village to watch and laugh. "What have you got there, Auntie? A new room for your house?"

The old woman would have liked to shout back some insult, but she knew she had to save her breath for the struggle. Mice from the rice, mice from the rice, she murmured to herself.

All the time she worked to get the jar up to the village, her neighbors just stood around and made jokes.

Mice from the rice, mice from the rice, she said over and over.

The old woman tried to ignore them, but by the time she reached the gates, her face was a scarlet red—as much from embarrassment as from the physical effort.

As she rolled the jar down her alley and into her house, she grunted. "Well, this isn't any Indian palace, but it's home." She set it upright against a wall. "I hope you're worth all the work."

She took her three coins and reburied them in the corner. Then she poured the rice into the big jar. The white grains tinkled against the sides. She turned her pouch inside out so that she wouldn't waste one grain. "Just keep the mice from the rice."

She felt so exhausted that she lay down on her straw mat and went right to sleep.

The next day when she woke up, she realized what a fool she was. "I'll run out of rice soon, and then I'll have to use my three cash to buy more rice. When that runs out, I'll have to go out begging. All that work to bring the big jar home, and I won't have anything to put into it."

Grumbling to herself, she went to the jar for that day's bowl of rice. But when she scooped out a handful, she was surprised to see how much rice was still on the bottom. She put her hand in and scooped out another handful. Curious, she looked inside. There was as much rice as before.

She put back most of the rice and cooked her bowlful. Then she had another bowl for lunch and a third for dinner.

But there were always the same two handfuls of rice at the bottom of the jar.

"It's magic." The old woman patted the jar wonderingly. "Thank you, friend."

She had three meals every day; and each time she peeked into the jar there were still two handfuls left at the bottom. The amount of rice never increased nor decreased. But she always took the precaution of thanking the jar.

But in a village your neighbors know almost everything about you—or if they don't yet, they soon will. They could see the smoke when the old woman cooked her meals. They knew she was poor and yet she ate three times a day. They began to spy on the old woman, and so one day a neighbor overheard her thanking the magic jar.

In no time, word of the magical jar spread throughout the village. People crowded into her little alley and pounded at her door. When she opened it, they demanded to see the magic jar, but the old woman refused. "You saw it the other day when I was rolling it up the path."

One neighbor wriggled his way into the front. "I'll give you ten pieces of silver for the jar."

A second neighbor shoved the first one out of her way. "He's cheap. I'll give you a hundred pieces of gold."

A third neighbor elbowed his way in front of the others. "I won't cheat you like them. We'll be partners. You provide the jar and I'll provide the gold to put into it. We'll split fifty-fifty."

The old woman shrugged. "What do I need with money now that the jar gives me food? Enough is enough. I have what I want."

"But you could be rich," the neighbor protested. "You're the contrariest woman in the whole country!"

The old woman just eyed all her greedy neighbors. "You all laughed at the jar. But magic is not mocked." She added, "And neither am I."

And she slammed the door shut—right in all their faces.

The Boasting Contest

"I COULD REALLY USE SOME HELP in the fields," Wong Three said to his two brothers.

Wong Two began to pat his little brother on the back and shoulders. "We will—just as soon as we finish practicing our kung fu."

Wong Three wasn't fooled for one moment. "You won't find my money on me."

"We're your brothers," Wong One said. "We're supposed to share everything." When he nodded to Wong Two, Wong Two wrapped his arms around their little brother's waist and turned him upside down.

"You won't find it there either," Wong Three said calmly. "You won't get drunk on my money."

"That's the thanks we get for protecting the village." Wong One pulled off his little brother's shoes. "We only have a few cash. Lend us some more."

"You're n-n-nothing b-b-but b-bullies," Wong Three said as Wong Two began to shake him up and down. "Y-you b-b-beat up an-n-nyone who tr-tries t-to sp-peak up-p."

Wong One looked at the floor, but no coins had fallen out. Taking their little brother from Wong Two, he hung up the youngest Wong on a hook. "It's peaceful, isn't it?"

With a laugh, the two older brothers left for the wine shop. It took a while for Wong Three to get down from the hook. He picked up his hoe. It was the last thing his two lazy brothers would touch. The cash were between the shaft and the head of the hoe.

With a sigh, he straightened his clothes and went on down to the fields. "I promised mother that I'd look after them. But sometimes it's hard."

When the two older brothers got to the wine shop, they found a wandering peddler sitting there. At his feet, he had the usual candies, toys, and odd knickknacks in two baskets at his feet. His carrying pole was over in a corner. On the table in front of him, he had a drum and a jar of wine.

The two brothers sat down, one on either side.

"How about a drink?" Wong One put on his fiercest glare.

But the stranger wasn't the least bit scared. He calmly poured himself a cup of wine. "I wouldn't insult you. The wine isn't what it used to be."

Wong Two tried to snatch the jar out of the stranger's hand, but the stranger was too strong. "Your kung fu is good," the middle brother had to admit.

The stranger sipped his wine. "I won't insult you either. Kung fu isn't what it used to be either."

Wong One knocked his cup idly on the tabletop. "That's

the truth. Nothing's like it used to be. My aunt made me a shirt and the cloth fell apart at the first washing."

"That," the stranger said, "depends on how many months you wore it without taking it off."

Wong Two eyed the stranger. The ones they couldn't bully they usually tried to trick. "You look like a man who's traveled places and seen a few things. Let's match stories."

The stranger thought about it. "Loser buys some noodles?"

Wong One nodded his head. "Done. The shop owner can be the judge. Though it's hardly worth the bother." He stretched out his legs to get comfortable. "The world's gotten worse and worse since I was a boy. Crops are poor; noodles are tough and thin. You can't count on anything. Not even drums."

He leaned forward and tapped the top of the stranger's drum. "Back when I was a boy, the priest had a drum that you could hear all around the province. The province? I mean, the world. We used to keep time by it. And when that priest beat the drum, people would stop whatever they were doing and listen to the wonder of it. It was a beat to make lions dance and dragons fly." He held up a wrist. "The blood pulsed to its beat." He lowered his hand. "But eventually that priest had to burn it."

"Why's that?" the stranger asked.

Wong One folded his arms. "Nobody was working while the priest beat the drum. No crops were grown. No meals were cooked."

The stranger kicked back his heels. "That reminds me of a buffalo I heard about once. It was big as this wine shop. It could turn over the soil in a whole valley in just one day; and when it bathed in a pond, it caused floods in the nearby villages. It was the wonder of four counties and Canton too, but eventually the buffalo owner had to kill it.''

"Why's that?'' Wong Two asked.

"It had such big lungs that you could hear it breathing all over the world.'' The stranger tapped the drum slowly in the rhythm of someone breathing. "People got their breathing all mixed up with the buffalo's. Three people suffocated because they forgot to inhale. They could hear the buffalo inhaling and they thought it was their lungs. But its meat fed the village for a year.'' The stranger sighed. "And they took the hide and made it into a drum. Gave it to a priest, I hear.''

The shop owner laughed loudly. He would have liked to have kept the two brothers out of his shop, but he was afraid of their fists. Now he had a chance to get even. "I think you owe the stranger some noodles.'' He held out his hand. "Money in advance, if you please.''

As Wong One grudgingly counted out the cash, the stranger poured himself another cup of wine. "I don't like the looks of those clouds. You don't know where I could sleep tonight?''

Wong Two saw their chance for revenge. "Friend, you could stay at our house, but the house leaks and there are bugs all over. Houses just aren't what they used to be.''

The stranger glanced out the window at the dark storm clouds. "Well, it wouldn't be the first time that I slept in the rain and had bugs crawl over me.''

Wong One chimed in. "And our little brother snores fiercer than a tiger roars. Little brothers aren't what they used to be either.''

Wong Two slapped his hand on the table. "I know. There's a house on the hill. They say it's haunted. Got a monster with a man's head and a dog's body. No one's ever stayed the night."

Wong One thought he understood his brother's plan. He nudged the stranger. "You look like you have the courage."

The stranger looked first at one brother and then at the other. "If it was worth my while."

Wong One nodded to him. "We'll bet you a dinner and wine that you won't stay the night."

"In this village they don't make gamblers like they used to either." The stranger laughed at them.

That only made the two brothers even angrier. "What do you want to wager?" Wong One asked.

The stranger thought about that for a moment. "All of us will go to the house. We'll each sleep in a separate room. If I don't stay the night, I'll be your slave. If either of you don't, you'll both be mine."

"And what if we all three stay in the house?" Wong Two asked.

The stranger smiled. "Then we'll prove that there are still people as brave as heroes in the old days."

Wong One gulped, but he wasn't the type to let anyone get the best of them—even if it was a fool's bet. "All right."

Wong Two agreed. "Right."

When the stranger had finished his meal, the two brothers led him up to the haunted house. It had once been a fine place with a large courtyard, but the walls had fallen down and weeds and bushes almost hid the house.

Inside, the house was dark as a landlord's heart. The wind whistled eerily through the eaves and the holes in the roof, but the stranger was very calm. "Sounds like the wind's changing. Monsoon should come in soon." The stranger set his things down and then lay on the floor. Resting his head on his drum, he put his straw hat over his face. "Wake me tomorrow."

Wishing the stranger a good night, the two brothers left his room.

Wong Three found them there. He held up his lantern to look at their faces. "I heard about your crazy bet. Call it off now and let's go home."

"We're not going to lose," Wong One nudged Wong Two. "We'll wait until he's asleep and then scare him into running out of the house and right into slavery."

"That's right." Wong Two pursed his lips together and made a strange whistling noise. Wong One growled and moaned eerily.

"I'd warn that poor peddler, except he sounds as crooked as you," Wong Three said. "Well, I'll be sitting by the gates when you get tired of your game." And the youngest brother went outside.

"That boy will never amount to anything," Wong One grunted.

Wong Two chuckled. "We should each go into a different room while we wait for him to fall asleep. That way he won't get suspicious."

Wong One poked his brother. "You're getting smart in your old age. It must be from hanging around me."

The two brothers went into different rooms to sit and wait. But after all the wine and the talking, the two brothers fell asleep. Wong One woke to see someone else was in the room.

"Brother," he called, "is that you?"

The figure drew nearer. When Wong One saw the drum around the person's neck, he knew it was the stranger.

Slowly, the stranger crouched on all fours. Underneath the hat, red eyes glowed.

"You cheat," Wong One said. "You're trying to scare us. The bet is off."

"You'll stay the night and every night." The stranger's hands and wrists stretched out until they were long and thin as a dog's paws. "Everything changes except for one thing." His shoes fell off with a plop from a rear set of paws.

Wong One could not take his eyes from the stranger as he backed away. "What's that?"

The stranger's back suddenly burst through his shirt to reveal black fur. He reared upward on a dog's hind legs. "Death always stays the same."

Wong One felt his back touch the crumbling plaster of a wall. "You don't want to eat me. I'm all skin and bones. My younger brother is plumper." He pointed a shaking finger at the next room.

The dog spirit studied Wong One. "That's true. But if he doesn't fill me up, I'm coming back for you."

And with a puff of smoke, he disappeared. As Wong One ran toward the gates, Wong Two woke.

He gave a scream when he saw the dog spirit. "Don't eat me," he said. "My little brother is a lot younger. He'll be sweeter and tastier. He's out by the gates."

The dog spirit considered that for a moment. "That's true. But if I don't like his taste, I'm coming back for you."

And he vanished from the room.

But when the spirit reappeared by the gates, there was

no sign of Wong Three. "Maybe he was the only smart one," the dog spirit muttered.

However, Wong Three had been cautious enough to hide. He had also been careful enough to bring some weapons with him. He stepped out now from behind the ruins of a wall. In one hand he had a long whip and in the other he had a big knife.

Before the dog spirit could do anything, Wong Three flicked his wrist, and the whip cracked through the air and wound itself around the neck of the dog spirit. With a jerk of the whip, the youngest brother pulled the spirit off his feet. The next moment he was on top of the spirit with his knife raised.

"Take my drum and spare me," the dog spirit coughed.

"That old thing?" Wong Three asked skeptically.

"Just make a wish and tap on the drum a few times," the dog spirit said desperately. "And you'll get what you want."

Wong Three carefully took the drum from around the dog spirit's neck and put it around his own. "I wish I and my two brothers were back at home," he said and beat his fingers on the drum. The next moment the haunted house vanished; and he and his two frightened brothers were standing in their own house.

Proudly, Wong Three showed them the drum and explained what had happened.

"It's not fair," Wong Two complained. "We take all the risks and he's the one who gets rich."

"I'll share it," Wong Three said. "My good fortune is our good fortune."

Wong One snorted. "You'll just lord it over us."

But Wong Two had an idea, and he whispered in the oldest brother's ear. "Let's get whips and knives too. Then we'll go back tomorrow night and get drums of our own."

The next night the two older brothers waited for their youngest brother to go to sleep. Then they armed themselves with the things they had gotten during the day and marched boldly into the haunted house.

The dog spirit suddenly appeared. He stood upright on two legs. Only his head was like a dog's. "I thought you two would come back." His red eyes glowed.

"Get him!" Wong One shouted, and sent his whip lashing around the dog spirit's neck.

Wong Two also coiled his whip around the dog spirit's neck. "We want magic drums too."

"And I want my dinner." The dog spirit pulled a knife from behind his back and cut first one whip and then the other.

"Run, brother!" Wong One said.

But it was already too late. And the dog spirit's dinner tasted all the sweeter and better for a night's delay.

In Chinese America

These are stories that may have had special appeal at one time or another among Chinese-Americans. Floods are frequent in California, especially along the delta and rivers where many of the Chinese lived and still live. Perhaps the flood-causing "Trouble Snake" helped explain their new situation overseas. Although the boy meant only to be kind to another creature, he was at fault for not obeying his mother.

Moreover, the Chinese provided the raw muscle that not only built railroad lines in the West and Southwest, but made the West's industry and agriculture possible. One can find the relics of Chinese America still—including enormous wine cellars that still bear the marks of their picks and the stone walls that they constructed. And perhaps the story "Breaker's Bridge" was told around the campfire or stove while laborers rested aching muscles.

Then, too, working in a labor gang would have required not only strength and endurance but loyalty as well. Virtue or Hsueh Yan Kui, the hero of "Virtue Goes to Town," was a soldier-cook who rose to be a general, and his and his descendants' exploits are popular material. And how did their families view these men when they returned from the Golden Mountain to China? Perhaps "The Homecoming" is an allegory of the power of love.

Trouble
Snake

ONE MORNING TWO BROTHERS were walking to school in the village. By a pond, the older brother saw a small snake sunning itself on a rock. It was a bright blue-green.

"It looks like a jeweled dagger," the older brother said. "I've never seen anything more beautiful."

But the little brother wouldn't go near it. "Mother told us all about that kind. It's a trouble snake for sure."

But the older boy didn't like to be told what to do—especially by his little brother. "This little fellow wouldn't hurt me." The trouble snake liked the warmth of his hand. It coiled around his fingers. "Well, aren't you the friendly thing? You don't want to let go, do you? Well, maybe I'll take care of you. Mother's always saying we should be kind to all living things—especially to something this pretty."

His little brother stepped back cautiously. "Mother also

says you can do the wrong things for the right reasons."

But the older brother could not part with the lovely snake. Instead, he dropped the trouble snake into a pouch and then held his fist up to his little brother. "If you tell Mother, you'll be doing the wrong thing for the wrong reasons. I'll hurt you so bad that you'll wish you had been bitten by a snake."

He took it to school, where he put it in a drawer of his desk; the snake curled right up and kept quiet. When school was over, he slipped it back into the pouch.

When he got home, he stole some rice when his mother wasn't looking. But his little brother was. The older brother just held up his fist in warning. His little brother instantly looked the other way. Then the older brother fed the rice to his pet.

Day after day, the older boy kept his pet with him and tended it carefully. And the snake would curl itself lovingly around his fingers. Gradually, the trouble snake grew and grew until it had to wrap itself around his arm instead. His little brother kept quiet and their mother never found out.

Eventually, it became too big for the pouch, so the older boy got a new pouch. But then came the day when the snake could not squeeze into the desk drawer no matter how it slithered and coiled.

Reluctantly, the brother took the trouble snake to the pond where he had found it. "Don't worry. I'll still visit you every day."

And each day, the older brother visited his pet and fed it so that the trouble snake continued to grow sleek and huge and even more beautiful. It became so large, in fact, that when they played, the snake could encircle the boy's entire chest.

But one day the little brother went to the pond. When he saw a duck, he decided to chase it. He splashed right into the pond until he was up to his waist in water. As he slapped his hands against the surface, the trouble snake came to investigate. Like a long, blue spear, it darted through the water. When it saw it was the little brother, it whirled around to go away. But its mighty tail lashed the little boy's legs.

With a cry, the boy fell over into the water. His head hit a rock and he drowned.

When the little boy did not return home, his mother and older brother went looking for him. They found the corpse floating in the pond. The trouble snake was nudging the body as if it were trying to wake it up.

The older brother instantly waded into the pond. "I was supposed to be the one to watch over you. But you were the smart one. Why didn't I listen to you? That really is a trouble snake."

When the trouble snake saw the older brother, it immediately came over to play. The mother screamed when she saw the huge snake begin to coil itself around his chest.

"It's all right. He won't harm me." The older brother gently fended off the trouble snake and drew his brother's body to shore.

When his mother demanded to know what he meant, the older brother had to tell his mother that he had kept the trouble snake as a pet.

The mother could hardly believe her ears. "You took

care of the snake that killed your brother?'' In a rage, the mother ran back to their house, snatched up a huge cleaver and came back to the pond.

The older brother sat weeping beside his little brother while the trouble snake lay coiled at his feet.

The mother raised the cleaver furiously. ''You took my boy's life. Now I'll take yours.''

Despite what his pet had done, the older brother kicked the trouble snake. ''Go into the deep part of the pond.''

The snake hurriedly slithered back into the water, but not quick enough. With an outraged scream, the mother brought the cleaver down and cut off the snake's tail.

She took the tail and she buried it with the younger brother. And she made sure that the older brother never went near the pond again.

But eventually, the mother grew old and she died. People were gathered in the house for the funeral when a young boy appeared. He had only one leg so he had to limp. People gasped and pointed, and the older brother looked up. The crippled boy was the spitting image of his little brother.

During the years, the trouble snake had continued to grow in size and magic until it had the power to take any form it wanted. It bowed its head to the corpse of its benefactor's mother and left. When the trouble snake reached the pond, it took its true form again and entered the water.

Once his mother was buried, the older brother started to visit his pet again. Even when he became very old, he continued to play with the trouble snake as if he were a young boy. When he died, the trouble snake took the shape of the little brother again and mourned at his grave. People would see the trouble snake visiting the grave as a small boy for many years after that.

Years became decades. Decades became centuries. During that time, the snake became even more powerful. But it was lonely and missed its old friend, so it decided to go to Heaven. It had gone half of the way when it was stopped by a boy with a big bracelet on one arm.

"You don't have any tail. Creatures can't go into Heaven only half dressed," the boy said.

Now in all this time, the trouble snake had become rather spoiled, so he tried to wriggle past. "Don't tell me what to do, boy. I'm pure trouble and twice as mean. I go where I want."

"You need a lesson in manners." The boy was no ordinary boy. He was a saint. He changed himself suddenly into a huge monster with three heads and three arms. They fought and wrestled all around the sky. Clouds were shredded like balls of cotton, winds whipped the fields and knocked down trees. The saint won.

"You haven't heard the last from me," threatened the snake. "I'll make so much trouble on earth that you'll want me up in Heaven." The trouble snake went back to the earth. It plunged into a river, where it whipped its tail about so that a flood spilled through the towns on the shore.

And after that, when a mighty tidal wave rolls in from the sea or a river jumps over its banks and levees, folk say it is the trouble snake trying to get into Heaven.

Breaker's
Bridge

THERE WAS ONCE A BOY who was always breaking things. He didn't do it on purpose. He just had very clumsy hands. No matter how careful he tried to be, he always dropped whatever he picked up. His family soon learned not to let him set the table or send him for eggs. Everyone in the village called him Breaker.

But Breaker was as clever as he was clumsy. When he grew up, he managed to outlive his nickname. He could design a bridge to cross any obstacle. No canyon was too wide. No river was too deep. Somehow the clever man always found a way to bridge them all.

Eventually the emperor heard about this clever builder and sent for him.

"There is a river in the hills," the emperor said to him. "Everyone tells me it is too swift and deep to span. So I

125

have to go a long way around it to get to my hunting palace. But you're famous for doing the impossible."

The kneeling man bowed his head to the floor. "So far I have been lucky. But there is always a first time when you can't do something."

The emperor frowned. "I didn't think you were lazy like my other bridge builders. You can have all the workers and all the materials you need. Build the bridge and you'll have your weight in gold. Fail and I'll have your head."

There was nothing for Breaker to do but thank the emperor and leave. He went right away to see the river. He had to take a steep road that wound upward through the hills toward the emperor's hunting palace.

It was really more than a palace, for it included a park the size of a district, and only the emperor could hunt the wildlife. The road to it had to snake through high, steep mountains. Although the road was well kept, the land became wilder and wilder. Pointed boulders thrust up like fangs, and the trees grew in twisted, writhing clumps.

Breaker became uneasy. "This is a place that doesn't like people very much."

The road twisted suddenly to the left when it came to a deep river gorge. On the other side of the gorge, the many trees of the palace looked like a dark-green sea. The yellow-tiled roofs looked like golden rafts floating on its top. Dark mountains, their tops capped with snow all year round, loomed behind the palace like monstrous guards.

Breaker carefully sidled to the edge of the gorge and looked down. Far below, he saw the river. When the snow melted in the distant mountains, the water flowed together to form this river. It raced faster than a tiger and stronger than a thousand buffalo. When it splashed against a rock, it threw up sheets of white spray like an ocean wave.

Breaker shook his head in dismay. "The emperor might as well have commanded me to bridge the sea."

But his failure would mean the loss of his head, so the next day Breaker set to work. The river was too wide to span with a simple bridge. Breaker would have to construct two piers in the middle of the river. The piers would support the bridge like miniature stone islands.

From the forests of the south came huge logs that were as tough and heavy as iron. From the quarries of the west came large, heavy stones of granite. The workers braved the cold water to sink the logs in the muddy riverbed. Breaker had to change the teams of workers often. The cold numbed anyone who stayed too long in the river.

Once the logs had been pounded into the mud, he tried to set the stones on top of the logs. But the river did not want to be tamed. It bucked and fought like a herd of wild stallions. It crushed the piles of stones into pebbles. It dug up the logs and smashed them against the rocky sides until they were mounds of soggy toothpicks.

Over the next month, Breaker tried every trick he knew; and each time the river defeated him. With each new failure, Breaker suspected more and more that he had met his match. The river flowed hard and strong and fast like the lifeblood of the earth itself. Breaker might as well have tried to tame the mountains.

In desperation, he finally tried to build a dam to hold back the river while he constructed the biggest and strongest piers yet. As he was supervising the construction, an official came by from the emperor.

"This bridge has already cost a lot of money," he announced to the wrecker. "What do you have to show for it?"

Breaker pointed to the two piers. They rose like twin towers toward the top of the gorge. "With a little luck, the emperor will have his bridge."

Suddenly, they heard a distant roar. The official looked up at the sky. "It sounds like thunder, but I don't see a cloud in the sky."

Breaker cupped his hands around his mouth to amplify his voice. "Get out," he shouted to his men. "Get out. The river must have broken our dam."

His men slipped and slid on the muddy riverbed, but they all managed to scrambled out just as a wall of water rolled down the gorge. The river swept around the two piers, pulling and tugging at the stones.

Everyone held their breath. Slowly the two piers began to rock back and forth on their foundations until they toppled over with a crash into the river. Water splashed in huge sheets over everyone, and when the spray finally fell back into the river, not one sign of the piers remained.

"All this time and all this money, and you have nothing to show for it." The official took a soggy yellow envelope from his sleeve.

Breaker and the other workers recognized the imperial color of the emperor. They instantly dropped to their knees and bowed their heads.

Then, with difficulty, Breaker opened the damp envelope and unfolded the letter. "In one month," it said, "I will have a bridge or I will have your head." It was sealed in red ink with the official seal of the emperor.

Breaker returned the letter and bowed again. "I'll try," he promised.

"You will do more than try," the official snapped. "You will build that bridge for the emperor. Or the executioner will be sharpening his sword." And the official left.

Wet and cold and tired, Breaker made his way along a path toward the room he had taken in an inn. It was getting late, so the surrounding forest was black with shadows. As he walked, Breaker tried to come up with some kind of new scheme, but the dam had been his last resort. In a month's time, he would feel the "kiss" of the executioner's sword.

"Hee, hee, hee," an old man laughed in a creaky voice that sounded like feet on old, worn steps. "You never liked hats anyway. Now you'll have an excuse not to wear them."

Breaker turned and saw a crooked old man sitting by the side of the road. He was dressed in rags, and a gourd hung from a strap against his hip. One leg was shorter than the other.

"How did you know that, old man?" Breaker wondered.

"Hee, hee, hee. I know a lot of things: the softness of clouds underneath my feet, the sound of souls inside bodies." And he shook his gourd so that it rattled as if there were beans inside. "It is the law of the universe that all things must change; and yet Nature hates change the most of all."

"The river certainly fits that description." Although he was exhausted and worried, Breaker squatted down beside the funny old man. "But you better get inside, old man. Night's coming on and it gets cold up in these mountains."

"Can't." The old man nodded to his broken crutch.

Breaker looked all around. It was growing dark, and his stomach was aching with hunger. But he couldn't leave the old man stranded in the mountains, so Breaker took out his knife. "If I make you a new crutch, can you reach your home?"

"If you make me a crutch, we'll all have what we want." It was getting so dim that Breaker could not be sure if the old man smiled.

Although it was hard to see, Breaker found a tall, straight sapling and tried to trim the branches from its sides; but being Breaker, he dropped his knife several times and lost it twice among the old leaves on the forest floor. He also cut each of his fingers. By the time he was ready to cut down the sapling, he couldn't even see it. Of course, he cut his fingers even more. And just as he was trimming the last branch from the sapling, he cut the sapling right in two.

He tried to carve another sapling and broke that one. It was so dark by now that he could not see at all. He had to find the next sapling by feel. This time he managed to cut it down and began to trim it. But halfway through he dropped his knife and broke it. "He'll just have to take it as it is," Breaker said.

When he finally emerged from the forest, the moon had come out. Sucking on his cut fingers, Breaker presented the new crutch to the funny old man.

The old man ran looked at the branches that grew from the sides of his new crutch. "A little splintery."

Breaker angrily took his cut finger from his mouth. "Don't insult someone who's doing you a favor."

The crooked old man lifted his right arm with difficulty

and managed to bring it behind his neck. "Keep that in mind yourself." He began to rub the back of his neck.

Breaker thrust the crutch at the old man. "Here, old man. This is what you wanted."

But the old man kept rubbing the back of his neck. "Rivers are like people: Every now and then, they have to be reminded that change is the law that binds us all."

"It's late. I'm tired and hungry and I have to come up with a new plan. Here's your crutch." And Breaker laid the crutch down beside the old man.

But before Breaker could straighten, the old man's left hand shot out and caught hold of Breaker's wrist. The old man's grip was as strong as iron. "Even the least word from me will remind that river of the law."

Breaker tried to pull away, but as strong as he was, he could not break the old man's hold. "Let me go."

But the crooked old man lowered his right hand so that Breaker could see that he had rubbed some of the dirt and sweat from his skin. "We are all bound together," the old man murmured, "and by the same laws." He murmured that over and over until he was almost humming like a bee. At the same time, his fingers quickly rolled the dirt and sweat into two round little pellets.

Frightened, Breaker could only stare at the old man. "Ar-ar-are you some mountain spirit?" he stammered.

The old man turned Breaker's palm upward and deposited the two little pellets on it. Then he closed Breaker's fingers over them. "Leave one of these at each spot where you want a pier. Be sure not to lose them."

"Yes, all right, of course," Breaker promised quickly.

The old man picked up the crutch and thrust himself up

from the ground. "Then you'll have what you want too." And he hobbled away quickly.

Breaker kept hold of the pellets until he reached the inn. Once he was among the inn's bright lights and could smell a hot meal, he began to laugh at himself. "You've let the emperor's letter upset you so much that you let a harmless old man scare you."

Even so, Breaker didn't throw away the pellets but put them in a little pouch. And the next morning when he returned to the gorge, he took along the pouch.

The canyon widened at one point so that there was a small beach. Breaker kept his supplies of stone and logs there. Figuring that he had nothing to lose, Breaker walked down the steep path. Then he took the boat and rowed out onto the river.

As he sat in the bobbing boat, he thought of the funny old man again. "You and I," he said to the river, "are both part of the same scheme of things. And it's time you faced up to it."

Although it was difficult to row at the same time, he got out the pouch with the two pellets. "I must be even crazier than that old man." He opened the pouch and shook one of the pellets into his hand.

When he was by the spot where the first pier should be, Breaker threw the pellet in. For a moment, nothing happened. There was only the sound of his oars slapping at the water.

And suddenly the surface began to boil. Frantically, he tried to row away, but the water began to whirl and whirl around in circles. Onshore, the workers shouted and ran to higher ground as waves splashed over the logs and stones.

From beneath the river came loud thumps and thuds and the grinding of stone on stone. A rock appeared above the surface. The water rose in another wave. On top of the wave another stone floated as if it were a block of wood. The river laid the first stone by the second.

Open-mouthed, Breaker watched the river lay stone after stone. The watery arms reached higher and higher until the first pier rose to the top of the gorge.

As the waters calmed, Breaker eagerly rowed the boat over to the second spot. At the same time that he tried to row enough to keep himself in the right place, Breaker reached for the pouch and opened it.

But in his hurry, his clumsy fingers crushed part of the pellet. He threw the remainder of the pellet into the water and then shook out the contents of the pouch. But this time, the river only swirled and rippled.

Breaker leaned over the side and peered below. He could just make out the pale, murky shape of a mound, but that was all. Even so, Breaker wasn't upset. His workers could easily build a second pier and meet the emperor's deadline.

So Breaker finished the bridge, and that summer the emperor reached his hunting palace with ease. When the emperor finished hunting and returned to his capital, he showered Breaker with gold and promised him all the work he could ever want.

However, winter brought deep snows once again to the mountains. That spring, when the snow thawed, the river grew strong and wild again. It roared down the gorge and smashed against the first pier. But the first pier was solid as a mountain.

However, the second pier had not been built with magic.

The river swept away the second pier as if it were nothing but twigs.

The bridge was repaired before the summer hunting, but the emperor angrily summoned Breaker to his hunting palace. "You were supposed to build a bridge for me," the emperor declared.

"Hee, hee, hee," laughed a creaky old voice. "He did, but you didn't say how long it was supposed to stay up."

Breaker turned around and saw it was the crooked old man. He was leaning on the crutch that Breaker had made for him. "How did you get here?" he asked the old man. But from the corner of his eye, he could see all the court officials kneeling down. And when Breaker looked back at the throne, he saw even the emperor kneeling.

"How can we serve you and the other eight immortals?" the emperor asked the crooked old man.

"We are all bound by the same laws," the old man croaked again, and then vanished.

And then Breaker knew the old man for what he truly was—a saint and a powerful magician.

So the emperor spared Breaker and sent him to build other projects all over China. And the emperor never regretted that he had let Breaker keep his head. But every year, the river washed away part of the bridge and every year it was rebuilt. And so things change and yet do not change.

Virtue
Goes
to
Town

AFTER VIRTUE HAD BURIED HIS PARENTS, he went to see the wise woman. "They say you can read a face like a page in a book. Tell me what my destiny is."

But the wise woman just kept sipping her tea. "What would you have? A quiet, happy life as a farmer? Or a life of sorrow and glory?"

"I hate being bored," Virtue said.

The wise woman studied his face a long time. She patted his shoulder sadly. "Then go into town."

When Virtue arrived there, he saw a long line of men. "I heard that town folk did the oddest things. Are you all practicing to be a fence?" he asked.

A townsman leaning against a wall looked at Virtue and then looked away again. But Virtue's voice was loud, and he was such a pest that the townsman finally said, "They're hiring workers, Turnip."

"The name's Virtue. And they can sign me up too. I left the farm to see the world and get rich." He got in line behind the townsman.

However, it was a hot, summer day and Virtue quickly became impatient. As he wiped at the sweat on his forehead, he shouted, "Hey, can't you go any faster?"

The foreman sat at his table in the shade. He ignored Virtue and went on just as slowly as ever.

"Hey, we're not getting any younger," Virtue yelled.

Still the foreman ignored him.

"Maybe he's deaf." Virtue started forward.

The townsman stuck out his arm. "Hey, Turnip, wait your turn."

"I told you. My name's Virtue. So why don't I just take you right with me, friend?" Virtue tucked his arm into the townsman's. The others were too afraid to say anything else, but everyone watched as he stomped up to the foreman.

"I can outplow a water buffalo and can harvest more than twenty folk," Virtue said.

The foreman took an instant dislike to Virtue. "You may be strong; but you're not that strong. No one likes a braggart."

"It's not bragging if you really can do it," Virtue said.

The foreman grunted. "I'm the boss here. I say how we do things. Get back there."

"Come on, friend." With a sigh, Virtue carried the townsman back to the end of the line.

It took most of the day before Virtue finally reached the

table. Virtue made a muscle for the foreman. "No job's too hard for me."

The foreman put down his brush and folded his hands over his big belly. "I have all of my work crew already. All I need is a cook. Can you do that?"

Virtue frowned. He thought a cook's job was beneath him, but times were hard and jobs were scarce. "Can I cook?" Virtue said. "I could cook a whale and fricassee a dragon."

The foreman twiddled his thumbs. He would have liked to turn Virtue away, but he needed a cook. "You only have to cook rice, dried fish and vegetables. I guess even you couldn't ruin that."

"Whatever I do, I always do well," Virtue promised. "I would make a better worker. But if you want me as a cook, then I'll be the best cook I can be."

The workers had to get up at sunrise, but Virtue had to get up even earlier to boil the water for their tea. Even so, he always had the tea poured and the cold rice served in bowls before the first man was up. He tried to have a friendly, cheerful word for each of the other workers. "Smile, friend," he would say to one. "We're keeping farm hours now—not town hours."

And to another, he would say, "We're all in this together, neighbor."

And to a third, he would grin. "Teamwork. That's how we do it on the farm."

But all the other men were from town. They never thanked him. In fact, they never spoke to him. Behind his back, they laughed and called him the loud-mouthed turnip.

Still, Virtue did not give up easily. "These townsfolk will come around once they get to know me."

At noon, he served them supper. Then, picking up a huge cauldron in each hand, he went down to the river. Each of the cauldrons could have held a half dozen men, but Virtue dipped them into the water and lifted them out as easily as if they were cups.

After making several trips, he would set the cauldrons of water on big fires. By sunset, they would be bubbling. When the work crew came back, they would wash before they sat down to eat their dinner.

But one noon, the other workers were delayed. Virtue got hungrier and hungrier as he smelled the food. Finally, he ate his bowlful of rice. Still, there was no sign of anyone. Virtue was so bored that the only thing he could think of doing was to eat another bowlful of rice and wait.

When no one had shown up yet, he began to feel sorry for himself. "I do my job, but no one appreciates me. So maybe I'll just have another bowlful. That'll show them."

When he had finished his third bowl, he looked at the cauldron simmering on the big fire. "This rice is going to get burned. I shouldn't let it go to waste." Bored and lonely, Virtue began to eat right from the cauldron. Before he knew it, he had finished the whole cauldron of rice.

Tired and dirty, the work crew finally came back to camp. They were angry when they found the empty cauldron. "Where's our food, Turnip?" they demanded angrily. But no one went too close to Virtue.

Virtue gave an embarrassed cough. "My name's Virtue."

They glared at him. "You're nothing but a big sack of wind. How do you expect us to work on empty bellies?"

Virtue brightened. "Since I ate all your lunch, let me do all your work. It's only fair."

The foreman got ready to fire Virtue. "One person couldn't meet our goals by himself."

"We take turns back on the farm. I'll do their work and they can do mine," Virtue said.

"You'll kill yourself," one of the work crew objected.

The foreman thought for a moment and then smirked. "Let him."

So Virtue left the others back in camp and marched off to work with the foreman. The foreman set a hard pace, but Virtue did not complain. By the end of the day, he had done all the work and more—much to the surprise of the foreman.

When Virtue came back, he shook his head when he saw the one pot of hot water. "You're supposed to have hot water for me. That wouldn't wash a cat's tail." And then he saw the pot of rice they had cooked for him. "I've done the work of twenty men. I've got the hunger of twenty men. That wouldn't even feed a mouse."

"We don't have enough firewood," one of the work crew said.

"Then I'll take care of it myself this time." Picking up an ax in either hand, he marched up to the nearest tree. In no time, he had chopped it into firewood. Then, taking the huge cauldrons, he went down to the river and filled them.

One cauldron he used for his rice. The other he used for his bath.

When he finally sat on the ground, he wolfed down the whole cauldron of rice. The others just watched in amazement. Virtue laughed. "I work hard, I eat hard, friends."

All this time, the foreman had been thinking. "You're not just bragging. You really can do the work of a whole crew." The foreman still didn't like Virtue, but it was more important to get the job finished. "Tomorrow you can do the work again."

But Virtue had learned a few things since he had left the farm. He winked at the rest of the crew. "We're all a team." He turned back to the foreman. "You're not going to fire them, are you?"

The foreman had been planning to do that very thing. Then he could pocket all the extra wages. But there was something in Virtue's look that made the foreman think again.

"No, they can be the cooks," the foreman said grudgingly.

One of the work crew grinned at Virtue. "No one will ever mistake you for a modest man, but your heart's in the right place." Then he bowed his head to Virtue. And one by one, the others did too.

And that was why there was only one worker but twenty cooks.

And even though Virtue went on to become a mighty warrior and general, he never lost his talent for making friends . . . and enemies.

The
Homecoming

O NCE THERE WAS A WOODCUTTER who minded every-one's business but his own. If you were digging a hole, he knew a better way to grip the shovel. If you were cooking a fish, he knew a better recipe. As his village said, he knew a little of everything and most of nothing.

If his wife and children hadn't made palm leaf fans, the family would have starved. Finally his wife got tired of everyone laughing at them. "You're supposed to be a woodcutter. Go up to the hill and cut some firewood."

"Any fool can do that." The woodcutter picked up his hatchet. "In the mountains there's plenty of tall oak. That's what burns best."

His wife pointed out the window. "But there's a stand of pine just over the ridgetop."

Her husband looked pained. "Pine won't sell as well. I'll

145

take my load into town, where folk are too busy to cut their own. Then I'll come back with loads of cash." With a laugh, he shouldered his long pole. After he cut the wood, he would tie it into two big bundles and place each at the end of the pole. Then he would balance the load on his shoulder.

Waving good-bye to his children, he left their house; but his wife walked right with him. "What are you doing?" he asked.

His wife folded her arms as they walked along. "Escorting you."

He slowed down by a boy who was making a kite out of paper and rice paste. "That thing will never fly. You should—"

His wife caught his arm and pulled him along. "Don't be such a busybody."

"If a neighbor's doing something wrong, it's the charitable thing to set that person straight." He tried to stop by a man who was feeding his ducks. "Say, friend. Those ducks'll get fatter if—"

His wife yanked him away and gave him a good shake. "Do I have to blindfold you? We have two children to feed."

"I'm not lazy," he grumbled.

She kept dragging him out of the village. "I never said you were. You can do the work of two people when no one else is around. You're just too easily distracted."

She went with him to the very edge of the fields and sent him on his way. "Remember," she called after him. "Don't talk to anyone."

He walked with long, steady strides through the wooded

hills. "I'll show her. It isn't how often you do something, it's how you do it. I'll cut twice the wood and sell it for double the price and come back in half the time."

Complaining loudly to himself, he moved deep into the mountains. I want just the right sort of oak, he thought to himself. As he walked along, he kept an eye out for a likely tree.

He didn't see the funny old man until he bumped into him. "Oof, watch where you're going," the old man said.

The old man had a head that bulged as big as a melon. He was dressed in a yellow robe embroidered with storks and pine trees.

Playing chess with the old man was another man so fat he could not close his robe. In his hand he had a large fan painted with drinking scenes.

The fat man wagged a finger at the old man. "Don't try to change the subject. I've got you. It's checkmate in two moves."

The funny old man looked back at the chessboard. The lines were a bright red on yellow paper, and the chess pieces were flat disks with words painted in gold on their tops.

"Is it now, is it now?" the funny old man mused.

The woodcutter remembered his wife's warning. But he said to himself, "I'm not actually talking to them. I'm advising them." So he put down his hatchet and pole. "Actually, if you moved that piece"—he jabbed at a disk—"and moved it there"—he pointed at a spot on the board—"you'd have him."

But the old man moved a different disk.

The fat man scratched the top of his bald head. "Now how'd you think of that?"

The woodcutter rubbed his chin. "Yes, how *did* you think of that?" But then he nodded his head and pointed to one of the fat man's disks. "Still, if you shifted that one, you'd win."

However, the fat man ignored him as he made another move.

"Well," the woodcutter said to the old man, "you've got him now."

But the old man paid him no more mind than the fat man. "Hmmm," he murmured, and set his chin on his fist as he studied the board.

The woodcutter became so caught up in the game that he squatted down. "I know what you have to do. I'll be right here just in case you need to ask."

Neither man said anything to the woodcutter. They just went on playing, and as they played, the woodcutter became more and more fascinated. He forgot about chopping wood. He even forgot about going home.

When it was night, the funny old man opened a big basket and lifted out a lantern covered with stars. He hung it from a tree and the game went on. Night passed on into day, but the woodcutter was as involved in the game now as the two men.

"Let's take a break." The old man slipped a peach from one big sleeve. The peach was big as the woodcutter's fist, and it filled the woods with a sweet aroma.

"You're just stalling for time," the fat man said. "Move."

"I'm hungry," the old man complained, and took a big bite. However, he shoved a piece along the board. When he held the peach out to the fat man, the fat man bit into it hungrily.

Alternating moves and bites, they went on until there was nothing left of the peach except the peach stone. "I feel much better now," the old man said, and threw the stone over his shoulder.

As the two men had eaten the peach, the woodcutter had discovered that he was famished, but the only thing was the peach stone. "Maybe I can suck on this stone and forget about being hungry. But I wish one of them would ask me for help. We could finish this game a lot quicker."

He tucked the stone into his mouth and tasted some of the peach juices. Instantly, he felt himself filled with energy. Goodness, he thought, I feel like there were lightning bolts zipping around inside me. And he went on watching the game with new energy.

After seven days, the old man stopped and stretched. "I think we're going to have to call this game a draw."

The fat man sighed. "I agree." He began to pick up the pieces.

The woodcutter spat out the stone. "But you could win easily."

The old man finally noticed him. "Are you still here?"

The woodcutter thought that this was his chance now to do a good deed. "It's been a most interesting game. However, if you—"

But the old man made shooing motions with his hands. "You should've gone home long ago."

"But I—" began the woodcutter.

The fat man rose. "Go home. It may already be too late."

That's a funny thing to say, the woodcutter thought. He turned around to get his things. But big, fat mushrooms had sprouted among the roots of the trees. A brown carpet surrounded him. He brushed the mushrooms aside until he found a rusty hatchet blade. He couldn't find a trace of the hatchet shaft or of his carrying pole.

Puzzled, he picked up the hatchet blade. "This can't be mine. My hatchet was practically new. Have you two gentlemen seen it?" He turned around again, but the two men had disappeared along with the chessboard and chess pieces.

"That's gratitude for you." Picking up the rusty hatchet blade, the woodcutter tried to make his way back through the woods; but he could not find the way he had come up. "It's like someone rearranged all the trees."

Somehow he made his way out of the mountains. However, fields and villages now stood where there had once been wooded hills. "What are you doing here?" he asked a farmer.

"What are you?" the farmer snorted, and went back to working in his field.

The woodcutter thought about telling him that he was swinging his hoe wrong, but he remembered what the two men had said. So he hurried home instead.

The woodcutter followed the river until he reached his own village, but as he walked through the fields, he didn't recognize one person. There was even a pond before the village gates. It had never been there before. He broke into a run, but there was a different house in the spot where his home had been. Even so, he burst into the place.

Two strange children looked up from the table, and a strange woman picked up a broom. "Out!"

The woodcutter raised his arms protectively. "Wait, I live here."

But the woman beat the woodcutter with a broom until he retreated into the street. By now, a crowd had gathered. The woodcutter looked around desperately. "What's happened to my village? Doesn't anyone know me?"

The village schoolteacher had come out of the school. He asked the woodcutter his name, and when the woodcutter told him, the schoolteacher pulled at his whiskers. "That name sounds familiar, but it can't be."

With the crowd following them, he led the woodcutter to the clan temple. "I collect odd, interesting stories." The schoolteacher got out a thick book. "There's a strange incident in the clan book." He leafed through the book toward the beginning and pointed to a name. "A woodcutter left the village and never came back." He added quietly. "But that was several thousand years ago."

"That's impossible," the woodcutter insisted. "I just stayed away to watch two men play a game of chess."

The schoolteacher sighed. "The two men must have been saints. Time doesn't pass for them as it does for us."

And at that moment, the woodcutter remembered his wife's warning.

But it was too late now.

Love

"Dream Flier" does not come from Lee's original collection, but the goddess, T'ien-Hou, was worshiped widely in the Chinese temples set up in California during the nineteenth century. Her filial piety still has a special appeal, and old-timers would have especially appreciated a child who worried about her traveling kin.

The only story in the original sixty-nine stories that was set in America was "Slippers." When an old-timer told a story about a devoted daughter such as the one in this story, he might be speaking of his own loneliness, for he himself would be lucky to see his family once every five years because he was unable to bring his own family over. And more recent arrivals might be thinking of families separated by World War II and subsequent events.

But in the back of the old-timers' minds would always be the matter of their own homecomings. Though they lived most of their lives in America, the land of the Golden Mountains, they referred to themselves ironically as "guests." How did their home villages view these "guests of the Golden Mountain"? These guests had been changed by their stay in America. Perhaps the story "The Changeling" is an allegory of the power of love.

And what did the guests feel when they returned home and found their villages changed by the very money they sent home, and themselves fossils from another time and culture? When they looked at their prosperous villages and their much-better-educated children and grandchildren, did they feel the same sense of loss as the hero in "The Rainbow People"?

The original tale was about a thief's strategems. However, as I began to retell it, it took on other dimensions. Guests were not the only ones to feel a sense of loss. Any Chinese-American who leaves the Chinatowns of the coast to live in the Midwest would understand that there is a price to pay that is more than the cost of the airplane ticket. But then it is a lesson that all wanderers learn when they leave home. Perhaps it should be regarded as a meditation upon history and the dragon that lies in each of us.

Dream
Flier

A GIRL WENT DOWN TO THE POND with her friends. In her arms she had a load of laundry to wash. Although her father and brothers were merchants, they took many risks to sail to faraway places.

Sometimes their junk would return with a hold full of ivory, sweet-smelling woods and even pearls the size of duck eggs. Other times, pirates stole everything. Once they even lost their ship. As a result, her family lived as simply as the others in their village. Mother and daughter tended their own house and even wove their own cloth for the family's clothes. And the other children treated her just like one of them.

As the girl strolled along with her friends, she looked beyond the pond toward the sea and said a little prayer for the safety of her father and brothers. She was so busy praying that she did not look where she was going.

"Look out. You're going to walk into the pond," one friend warned her.

The girl looked down, but instead of going into the water, she stood on top of it. The others were silent as they stared at the wonder. The girl uncomfortably shuffled back to the land. The water felt slippery, like waxed wood, but it supported her weight easily.

"How did that happen?" She gave a nervous little laugh.

But all her friends were still looking at her. "Stop that," she said to them.

They edged away from her. "Careful, she might cast a spell," another of them whispered.

"I don't know any magic," she protested.

When her friends still kept their distance, she threw down her bundle of laundry and ran up the hill to her home. Weeping, she told her mother about the strange thing that happened.

The mother took her in her arms and rocked back and forth with her. "Magic fills the world, and yet the rich and the wise may spend all their wealth and lives seeking it and find nothing. But magic will leap unexpectedly upon others like a tiger on a lamb. Magic seizes whom it will. And no one knows how or why."

"But I don't want to be different," she wept.

The mother sighed, but she could give her no real comfort. "It's your gift, and it's your curse. You simply have to live with it."

"It's hard," the girl said.

The mother petted her cheek. "This may be the hardest thing I'll ever ask of you, but you have to listen to me."

Children of that time and place always tried to do what

their parents said—even if they did not always succeed. Obedience was the most important virtue.

"I will," the girl promised in a small voice.

Then, outside their house, they heard the voices of the fishermen as they walked to their homes.

"They're back early," the girl said.

They went outside in the street and looked down the hill from their house toward the bay. Many boats had already beached. More little fishing boats scuttled into the bay like bugs. The waves rolled and crashed noisily against the sand and black clouds swept in from the sea. "Any sign of our ship?" they asked the returning fishermen. But no one had seen their family's junk.

Finally, the two of them were left alone on the hill.

The girl bit her lip in worry. "Their ship is overdue, and now there's a storm coming in."

"Don't think about it." Her mother made her come back inside their house. "Help me with the little ones," her mother said. "The big ones will have to take care of themselves."

So the girl returned to her house, fed her younger brothers and sisters, and put them to bed. Her mother went to bed, but the girl could not sleep. She lit a candle and sat down at her loom. The long threads gleamed like dark hair in the soft light.

The loom clicked and rattled rhythmically. The girl's head began to nod drowsily. She felt as if her body were being spun into cotton threads, finer and finer, thinner and thinner until the threads were spread across the stars themselves, and she was the night sky itself.

But she became aware of a small part of herself. It was flying in the night like some seabird with great wings. She had only to bring her arms down in one powerful beat and she sped along. She was so high in the air that the storm clouds below merely looked like dirty cotton.

Suddenly she thought she heard her father cry out. Without hesitating, she plunged down into the dangerous storm clouds. It was dark all around her. The winds pulled and shoved at her. Cold numbed her arms and moisture made her clothes weigh as heavily as lead. Then one strange moment she felt a prickling sensation in her skin.

When she burst out of the storm clouds, the rain stabbed at her like hundreds of little arrows. Even so, she spiraled down, down, down until she saw the junk. From that height, it looked like a little chip of wood.

As she flew closer, she heard her father shout out again. She flew lower still. The sails were all gone, and the rudder was broken so the junk spun and bobbed like a toy. Then she saw her father and brothers clinging to the shattered mast.

She hovered over them. "Climb onto my back," she tried to say, but the wind drove the rain and seawater into her mouth. She coughed and spat and spoke again.

"Climb on." Although she was far smaller than any of the men, she was able to take one brother under her right arm and her other brother under her left. Then she caught hold of her father's collar between her teeth.

With a kick of her feet, she rose into the air. Beneath they heard a groan as the junk broke in two. In an instant, the sea swallowed up both halves.

Suddenly the sea sent huge waves skyward, trying to snatch her brothers from her arms, but she managed to climb out of its reach. It was difficult to rise with the heavy load through the rain. It was even harder once they were in the storm clouds. But somehow she struggled above them. She had just turned toward home when she heard her mother calling as if from a great distance.

"Be a good girl now. Wake up and come to bed," her mother said softly.

And what could the girl do? She had always obeyed her mother before. She opened her mouth and said, "Wait, mother." But her father's collar slipped from her teeth. She tried to catch him, but he fell screaming back into the clouds. If she dove after him, she would lose her brothers as well.

Her tears mixing with the raindrops, she flew on. The wind howled and blew at her. Dozens of giant hands seemed to shove her back.

But the girl was determined not to drop her brothers. She fought both wind and wave. Despite all the noise, she could hear her mother calling to her insistently. However, this time the girl did not answer. Instead, she struggled to the shore. She left her exhausted brothers safely on the sand.

The next moment, she could feel her mother shaking her shoulder gently. "Come on now. You've fallen asleep at the loom."

Opening her eyes, she saw that she was back in her own house. She looked down at her clothes. They were dry. "I had the strangest dream. Father died."

The mother stepped back in surprise. "Watch your tongue, girl."

But the girl told the mother about her dream. "I was able to save my brothers, but not father. . . ."

Her mother patted her on the shoulder. "It was just a bad dream. Now come to bed." And she helped her daughter get up from the loom and then put her to bed.

The next day they got word from her two brothers. They were on a point of land to the south, and they made their way home. But there was never a sign of her father nor of his junk.

After her death, the girl became the special protector of sailors and all those who venture on the sea. From the highest to the lowest, they sought her protection. A fisherman in a boat hardly bigger than a coffin would pause at the mouth of a bay and murmur a prayer to the girl who could walk on water. And when sailors on the huge ocean-going junks saw dark, angry clouds on the horizon, they would burn her picture and ask the aid of the girl who could safely fly through storms.

Slippers

YEARS AGO IN CHINA, there was a poor couple who had no children. They prayed often, but they were in their fifties before Heaven heard them and sent them a little girl.

They loved her all the more because having a child had once seemed so impossible. They even called her their miracle child. But when she was still very small, her mother died, and she, despite her youth, took over the household.

"She'll kill herself with work," the other villagers scolded her father.

Her father threw up his hands in frustration. "I know that. You know that. But I can't get her to stop. Once she sets her mind on something, she does it."

Every day her father would come home from the fields. He would wash the dust off; he would put on his favorite slippers. They would slap against his heels as he walked to

163

his chair. Then, with a sigh, he would sit down and prop his feet up.

"If you have a comfortable pair of slippers," he liked to say, "you can feel like a king."

She shook her head. "Your royal slippers are falling apart. You need new ones."

Her father stared down at his raggedy slippers. "They're like me, getting on in years. But we've grown comfortable together."

She picked up her needle. "I'll start now."

"You should be making them for your husband," her father said. "It's time you were married, and I think I have just the man. He's a guest of the Golden Mountain, with his own store over there. I've talked to other people, and he seems like a good person. He's willing to come back to China to marry you."

"But who'll take care of you?" the daughter wondered tearfully.

"I'm an old man with almost all of his life behind him," her father said in exasperation.

"I would give up some of my own life to extend yours," the girl said.

The father shushed her. "You never know what spirits might be listening." He studied her for a moment and then nodded. "If you feel that way, I'll try not to leave you. But you have to get married."

"Yes," the daughter promised.

But her father was very old and died before she could finish the new pair of slippers. The daughter put on the white of mourning and buried her father.

Life became very hard for her after that. Although she worked in the fields all day, she was a tenant farmer, so most of what she grew went to her landlord. As a result, she had very little to eat. Every night, to forget her hunger, she would work on her father's slippers. Because she could not even afford lamp oil or candles, she worked by the light of the moon.

Finally she put the last stitch into the phoenixes embroidered on the slippers. They were the finest she had ever made, but she refused to sell them. Instead, she left them in her father's room along with his other things. She was going to throw out his old slippers, but she couldn't part with them either. So she left both pairs of slippers side by side.

That night she woke up to a strange noise. *Slap. Slap. Slap.*

Monsters did not frighten her one bit. She got up from her sleeping mat and lit a candle. She looked all around the house and the kitchen but saw nothing.

She heard the slapping noise other nights, and always at the same time. She always got up and looked all over the house, but she never found anything.

A few months later, the guest left the land of the Golden Mountain and returned to China. She met him under the watchful eye of the matchmaker.

"I know I'm not as exciting as most men," the guest said. "I don't smoke or drink or gamble. But you'll find me steady enough. I like nothing better than to sit down in my favorite chair with a pair of slippers on my feet."

"And do you feel like a prince then?" the woman asked.

"I suppose I could," the guest smiled, "with the right woman. Make me a pair of your famous slippers. That's all I want as your dowry."

The matchmaker looked shocked, but the woman was beginning to like this guest. "I thought you were smarter than that."

"I'm smart enough to know quality. And that's what you are. You were loyal to your father, and you'll be loyal to your husband."

And he began to tell her about his travels and the land of the Golden Mountain.

"I've never been farther than ten kilometers in my life," she said thoughtfully. "It would be exciting to travel and see new lands."

"Then marry me," the guest said.

She shook her head. "People would say I was just marrying you to end my troubles."

"If you marry me, it won't be all that easy," he said. "There aren't many women over there. It can be lonely for a wife overseas. The Americans make it hard for Chinese to bring their wives over."

"Then how come you can do it?" she asked.

"I own a store," the guest explained. "That puts me in a different class."

"When you're the only child of elderly parents," she said, "you get used to being on your own."

The guest just grinned. "I knew you were quality when I saw you."

One meeting led to another. Before she knew it, the woman had come to love the guest. She made a new pair of slippers and gave it to him. They were married shortly afterward. Then she packed up her father's things and stored them away.

It was not as hard as it had once been to reach America, but it was still difficult. It was even harder to get into America. She was questioned closely. But her husband could hire the best American lawyers, so eventually she was freed.

He led her into Chinatown—a strange place. There were American buildings to which the Chinese had added their own decorations—balconies and shutters and other things. But it was still like seeing a strange face in Chinese costume.

And from there they journeyed on a boat far into the middle of the province to a tiny Chinatown of a few buildings. Beside their store, one was a temple and meeting place. Another was a restaurant. And two were buildings where the Chinese workers slept.

She was the only woman for twenty kilometers. The loneliness and strangeness were terrible things—like shadowy monsters that clutched at her. But even so, she refused to give in. She busied herself unpacking her trunk and rearranging the house to suit her taste.

But that night, as she lay on the odd American bed with her husband, she could not sleep. The loneliness closed in on her again. She listened to the alien insects and smelled the strange, new flowers outside her window. And she felt terribly homesick.

But then she heard a familiar sound that made her even more homesick. *Slap. Slap. Slap.*

"What's that?" Her husband lit the American kerosene lantern, and together they searched the whole store, but there was no one there.

"I used to hear it in China too," the woman said.

Her husband scratched his head. "I would have sworn I heard the sound of slippers slapping at someone's heels."

There in the middle of their parlor on the second story was a pair of old slippers.

"He kept his promise. He was coming back all this time, but I didn't understand it." She picked up her father's slippers from the floor and put them in their bedroom. And she didn't feel nearly so alone.

And after that at the same hour every day she would hear the slapping sound of her father's slippers.

The
Changeling

Oඖ EVENING TOWARD SUNSET, a farmer broke the dike around one of his fields. The dirty water rushed into the drainage ditch. In the field, the rice plants would dry and ripen for the harvest. As water gurgled and bubbled past, he looked about the valley. Dozens of little fields lay like bright, shining patches under the sunset. Tomorrow, he might plant some vegetables on the sides of the dikes.

Behind him, he could hear the voices of the other farmers as they went home. Their voices merged into a drowsy murmur. He turned and began to follow them along the dikes.

Suddenly an invisible blanket seemed to fall over him. He could see nothing, but something weighed at his head and arms. He tried to throw it off as icy claws felt his muscles—like someone feeling a chicken for butchering.

He opened his mouth to scream for help. In the distance, he could see the others trailing along the road to the village. But no sound came from his throat. Instead, he heard a loud babbling from all around him. He tried to lift his legs so he could run, but the invisible blanket weighed him down even more. He could only stand there while the voices grew louder and louder around him until they were roaring like the sea.

Dozens of paws lifted him off the ground; and they swept him toward the horizon faster and faster, higher and higher through the night sky toward a faraway mountain.

The farmer's wife waited for several hours. He sometimes worked long after the others did. But when he did not return by the next sunrise, she went out into the village street and began to cry for help. "My husband's gone. Something terrible's happened to him."

People, half dressed and half awake, tumbled out of their houses. Wiping at her tears, the worried woman told her story. Some of the villagers murmured to one another in fright, but an old man tried to calm her. "Don't assume the worst. He wouldn't be the first person to get tired of things and leave." The old man looked around and several heads nodded in agreement. "Does he fight with you?"

"We have our share of fights," the wife admitted, "but we always make up."

"Then you probably will again," the old man declared. "Let's let him come back in his own time."

The woman tried to argue, but now everyone else believed that her husband had run off. So the wife went down to search the fields herself. Her husband's hoe was right there where he had dropped it. Alarmed, she brought it back to the old man. But he patted her on the shoulder and insisted that her husband had simply left it.

That next morning, she woke the village. Sleepily, the villagers looked around the valley, but there wasn't a trace of her husband.

"You see." The old man yawned. "There isn't a single drop of blood or any sign of a struggle. He's gone off like I said. He'll be back when he's worked off his anger."

"You're all fools," the wife declared, and went to the next village to visit a wise man.

He could look at the hills and read them as a scholar reads a book; he knew many strange things. When the wife explained her worries to him, he did not speak. Instead, he closed his eyes and stretched the fingers of his right hand over a vase of sand. His forehead wrinkled as if he were deep in thought. Suddenly, his eyes blinked open.

He sighed and shook his head sadly. "Dear, dear, dear, this is a sorry mess. I wish you'd come to me earlier. A gang of evil ghosts has kidnaped your husband. If you want to find him again, you will have to send drummers through the hills. Your husband will appear when he hears them."

The wife went right back home and told her village what the wise man had said. Although the villagers were sorry, they told her they could not take that much time away from their fields.

But this time the determined woman would not let them go to their homes. "I listened to you before even when I knew better. But not anymore. I know what will save my husband, and I'm not about to give up."

And she scolded and threatened and even begged until she had a dozen drums and a dozen strong men to beat those drums.

"We can't stay out forever," the first drummer said. "Three days is all we can do."

"Then, with Heaven's mercy, that will be enough," the wife said, and she sent them out.

For two days and two nights, they trudged through valleys and up hills like a small, walking thunderstorm.

By the third day, their arms were tired and their feet were sore. "Let's go home," a second drummer said.

"We promised her three days." The first drummer pointed to a distant mountain. "Let's go as far as there and then we can go home."

The others felt sorry for the wife, and being honest souls, they agreed to keep their word. Although they were tired, they drummed loudly as they went.

As they neared it, they could see the mountain's sides were made of yellow clay. The second drummer slowed down. "They say that clay has the magic to change things."

"That's only a story," the first drummer said, and they began to climb up the steep sides. The path slanted up sharply and it was slippery to walk on, so they quickly grew tired. One by one, they stopped drumming. By the time they reached the top, only one of them was thumping his drum.

There, at the very top of the mountain, grew a solitary tree. Its trunk twisted and writhed like smoke. Its roots lay exposed above the dirt, arching and curling like a nest of snakes. The first drummer simply beat slowly at his drum while he stared at it. None of them had ever seen a tree like this.

Curious, the band of drummers edged toward the tree. The first drummer's mind was taken up with the strange tree, and he beat absentmindedly at his drum. Suddenly, there came an answering boom from the tree and a strange, apelike creature poked its face from the leaves. Its fur was a soft ruddy gold and its muzzle and face were a bright blue.

The drummer was so surprised, he hit his drum again. The ape opened its mouth and emitted another booming sound. The other drummers were ready to drop their drums and run away, but the first drummer peered at the creature. "That ape looks familiar. That nose and those beady eyes. That looks like the missing man."

The creature hung from a branch. Long, fine hair grew all over its body. "What's happened to him?" the second drummer wondered.

"I don't know, but we're supposed to bring him back," the first drummer said.

While one of them kept an eye on the creature, the others wove a crude net from vines. Then they hung the net on one part of the tree and picked up their drums again.

"One, two, three." The first drummer banged on his drum at the same time as all the others did.

As the thunderous noise rolled across the mountain top, the creature panicked and tried to escape. Instead, he ran right into the net. Once the men had the creature in the net, it stopped struggling and simply lay there, shaking.

When the second drummer got a closer look, he saw

that there was yellow clay in its ears and around its lips. "Someone or something's been feeding him the clay. I think we found him just in time, before they could complete the change."

The men hastily left the mountain before the ghosts came back. They took turns carrying the creature in the net. As they entered the farmer's valley, curious folk trailed them, careful not to get too close.

By the time they had reached the farmer's little house, there was a regular parade behind them. The first drummer rolled his sticks across the surface of his drum. "We've found him."

The door flew open and the wife ran out with open arms, but she stopped dead in her tracks when she saw the creature in the net. Frightened, she began to back up. "What do you mean? That monster isn't my husband."

The first drummer pointed one of his sticks at the creature. "Look closer."

Shuffling step by step, the woman neared the creature. When it saw her, it gave out a small, sad whimper.

She put her hands to her mouth. "It's him."

The second drummer scratched his head with a drumstick. "I suppose we could always build a cage for you."

The wife drew herself up. "He'll live in his house with me like he always has, and maybe he'll become his old self."

"And if he doesn't?" the first drummer asked.

"At least he'll be happy."

So the wife took the creature into their house. Day by day, she went to the temple and burned incense and asked Heaven to restore her husband. And day by day, she took care of the creature. She fed him and talked to him soothingly and saw to his wants.

Perhaps it simply took a while for the magic of the yellow clay to wear off, or perhaps it was simply the gentle caring. In either case, the creature shed more and more of its fur each day, and each day it stood a little straighter and looked more like a human.

And finally one morning, the wife woke up to see her husband kneeling beside her. "You're finally back," she said, and began to weep.

And seeing her cry, her husband began to weep as well. "Yes, I'm back. And thank you."

The
Rainbow
People

THE FISHERMEN TOLD HIM NOT TO GO to the mountain. "It's magical," they said. "A powerful wizard lives up there."

However, the wanderer was young, so nothing frightened him. "I said I'd play my flute in every part of the country and I will."

He took the path that led up from the beach. But the path had its own sense of humor, and it twisted and wound along the cliffsides until it dumped him back on the sand.

The fishermen were laughing. "We told you the mountain was magical."

"What this path needs is a little seriousness." The wanderer took a little wooden flute from his raggedy sash and he began to play. It was a song sad enough to make a pine tree droop like a willow and the sun go home and cry.

When he was finished, all the fishermen were lying flat

on their bellies and weeping like babies, and the path lay just as low and smooth as the fishermen.

Satisfied, he stuck the flute back into his sash and climbed the path into the mountain. The rocks were all limestone, and the rain and the sea had carved them into strange shapes. Some were like big white pine cones, but the higher he went, the more he felt like he was being watched. Then he realized that the rocks looked like the heads of animals. Here and there bushes clung to them like green fur.

Halfway up the mountain, though, the path entered a valley that had been carved out by a stream before it plunged over a cliff into the sea.

The cold mountain water fed fields of rice with grains as big as his fingers and vegetables with leaves as tall as him. But the people who tended them were the thinnest, boniest people he had ever seen.

He stopped by the nearest farmer. "How've you been eating?" the wanderer asked.

The farmer didn't say anything. He didn't even look up. He just went on with his weeding. Only he didn't stick the weeds into the dirt. Instead, he yanked them out and saved them in a basket.

The wanderer slipped out his flute and gave it a little toot. "I'll play for my supper."

"We work for ours," the farmer said.

"Music's food for the soul, and I serve up a banquet," the wanderer said. Raising the flute to his lips, he began to play. He made imaginary birds come down and wheel around his head, and the water sparkle on a hot summer day. When he was finished, he put down his flute. "You can pay me what you think it's worth."

"We don't think much. We work," the farmer said.

At first the wanderer was speechless. He had traveled all around and his flute had always made him welcome. But not here.

"You can have some of my meal," a voice said. It was low and soft like dark velvet.

Pivoting, he saw a girl who looked about his age. Even though she was short, she was swinging a hoe as big as she was. The perspiration had made her bangs stick to her forehead, but he could make out a birthmark there, a circle round as a pearl.

"We're not mean," she said. "But we have less than other folks."

"I don't ask for charity." He stepped down into the field beside her. "I'll earn my meal."

As little as she was, she looked up at him. "You work as long as you can, and then you sit down where you can't get in my way."

He smiled. "I'll work as long as you do."

"We'll see." She handed him the hoe.

The wanderer wasn't afraid of work. In his travels, he'd dug in the dirt and cut stone and laid bricks. But he'd never worked with people who went right through noon. They didn't stop for food. They didn't stop for water. In fact, they didn't stop for anything.

As hard as the wanderer tried, he couldn't keep up with the smallest child. He went off among the rocks and watched the others work. He was glad when the sun began to dip behind the mountain. Well, he thought to himself, they've got to stop now.

But as the twilight filled the valley, the farmers' faces

began to shine with soft, colored lights—as if they were wearing rainbows. It was so lovely that, even though the wanderer was right in the middle of magic, he wasn't the least bit frightened.

Even then, the rainbow people did not leave the fields. Instead, they went on working by the light they gave off. They stayed in the fields well into the night before they finally had their meal. However, they didn't go into the huts on one side of the valley. They just sat down in the fields.

Each of them received a bowl, and when the tired wanderer sat down with the girl, he saw that the bowl held a watery soup made with rice and green weeds. Now he knew why the farmers saved their weeds.

"Here." The girl held the bowl out to him. "You can have the first taste."

But the wanderer waved his hand at the big vegetables. "You're the best farmers I've ever seen. How come this is all you eat?"

"Because the landlord takes everything else." She shoved the bowl at him. "If you're not going to take the first taste, I will."

The wanderer motioned her to go ahead. "Landlords are mean, but I've never heard of one that mean. He must have a heart the size of a pebble."

She took a sip and then handed the bowl to him. "He doesn't have a heart. He's a wizard." She nodded toward the top of the mountain. "He lives up there in an old banyan tree."

He took a sip and then gave the bowl back to her. "Just because he's got all that magic doesn't mean he can push folks around."

She shook her head sadly. "We've tried and we've tried, but we can't break his magic."

All around him, the folks were piling up the bowls and going back to work. And he knew the girl was going to have to go back to work too. Men, women, children—everyone had to slave away in the fields. "Someone should have a talk with this wizard," he cried.

"Just go back the way you came," she said. "Or you'll get hurt." The light flickered all around her as if she were worried.

"Even landlords should be neighborly." The wanderer got up from the field, dusted off his pants, and went back to the path. All the rainbow people were watching him.

Grinning, he waved good-bye and walked up the path to its very end. There, the moonlight gleamed off the round mountaintop as if it were a giant skull. Nothing grew on the limestone except a huge, old banyan tree springing right out of the stone.

Its roots were bent like legs ready to dance, while vines with big green leaves wound around its trunk. And the air was thick with the smell of flowers even though there wasn't one in sight.

The wanderer crept up to the tree as quiet and easy as a cat. When he peered inside the tree, he saw that vines had been woven in and out among the roots, and a heavy, sweet scent came from the flowers drooping along the vines. Peeking through a space between the vines, he saw that the hollow tree was filled with a soft light coming from glass globes filled with glowing worms.

A dozen little men ran around in shoes of folded bark and robes like giant flowers of every color, and each of the little men had a wicked-looking knife. Some of them were cleaning up dinner dishes in a pail of water. Others were taking a light silk robe from a chest of carved black teak. Still others were standing guard around a long, narrow brass box. Over their heads an old bronze gong was hanging behind the box.

On top of the box was the wizard with green moss for hair. He was wearing a black robe with words sewn in silver thread so that the lettering looked like wriggling worms. Despite the big robe, he looked as old and chunky as his home.

"No, you stupid things," he said. "I want the satin robe with the fur collar. It's going to be cold tonight." His voice rasped like dusty rocks grating against one another.

The little men took out a velvet robe.

"I said satin. Do I have to do everything?" The little men scurried away as the wizard seemed to drift over the ground to the chest.

When the wizard took off his black robe, the wanderer could see that the wizard had dozens of legs just like his tree. And around the wizard's neck was a little brass key.

"I bet that's to the brass box," the wanderer murmured. "I wonder what's inside."

Then the wizard took out a slick, green robe with a dark fur trimming the collar and the sleeves. "This"—the wizard shook the robe—"this is satin."

When he had put on the robe, the wizard glided back to the box and gathered the little men around him. "You be ready to come as soon as I call. Now go away."

Picking up a red stick, he hit the gong. Even before

the crashing note had died, the little men had vanished. Then, lying down on top of the box, the wizard went to sleep.

The wanderer waited awhile before he pulled some of the vines apart and snuck inside the tree. The wizard was still on top of the box, his breast as still as stone. He was sleeping deep and quiet as seed in the ground.

Feeling bolder, the wanderer poked and pried at the box. But there was no way to get into it while the wizard was sleeping on top.

So carefully, ever so carefully, he took down the gong and hung the pail of water in its place. Unwinding the sash from around his waist, he stuck the gong and his flute back in the waistband of his pants. Then the wanderer unraveled the sash so that he had a long thread. He tied this around one of the wizard's ankles.

Then, leading the string over to the big chest, he got inside and lowered the lid. But when he pulled the thread, the wizard didn't do anything. So the wanderer tugged on the thread again. Still the wizard slept. The third time the wanderer yanked so hard the thread broke. But the wizard finally felt it.

"Help! Murder! Thieves!" shouted the wizard.

The wanderer risked a peek from underneath the lid and he saw the wizard jump up. Right away the wizard grabbed the red stick and gave the pail of water a whack that was strong enough to knock it from the wall and splash dirty dish water all over him and his fancy robe.

The wizard used the red stick to poke at the moss on his head. "Now how did that get there? And where's my gong?"

He looked all around the room, and the wanderer hurriedly ducked down.

Suddenly the wizard gave a sneeze. "I better change first before I catch a cold."

The wizard shuffled over to the chest. He moved noisily—like a small crowd trying to sneak up on someone. The wanderer waited and waited, and when the wizard raised the lid, the wanderer straightened up.

The wizard was standing there with one hand on the chest lid and the other holding up his dripping robe. "Who are you?" he asked.

"Am I in your way?" the wanderer asked, and tugged at the brass key around the wizard's neck. With a snap, the gold chain broke. Right away, the wanderer leaped out of the chest. But the gong fell out of his pants into the chest.

Running over to the box, the wanderer stuck the key into the lock.

"Get away from there." Dropping his wet robe, the wizard lifted out the gong, but he had hung the red stick back up on the wall. He had to hit the gong with his fist. "Ow, ow, ow! Come out, come out, come out." Each time his fist struck the gong, a dozen little men with sharp knives popped out of the air.

The wanderer twisted the key in the lock so that there was a click. I'm in for it now, he thought to himself. Whatever's inside the box had better be good.

Jerking the lid up, he looked inside. There, resting on red velvet, was a long golden flute. Etched on its side was a giant, dark warrior dancing on the back of a monstrous turtle. The wanderer only had time to snatch it up before the little knives were slashing at him.

Ducking and jumping, he put the gold flute in his mouth while he drew out his old flute. He didn't want to risk the gold one until he could figure out what made it so special.

"Carve him into a turnip," the wizard yelled.

But the wanderer was thrusting and swinging his old flute like a sword. Sometimes he knocked one of the little men on top of the head. More often, he had to parry a knife blade. Soon, his poor old flute was as notched as a comb. He began to pant for breath, and as his chest started to heave up and down, the gold flute gave a little whistle.

"Ge-e-t him," the wizard hiccuped.

From the corner of his eye he saw the wizard give a hop. And the little men all around him gave little skips. Curious, the wanderer blew harder on the flute and the wizard began to lift and kick one foot after another while little men skipped about.

The wanderer started to finger the flute. Instantly, the wizard stomped and circled. As the little men began to whirl around him, the wizard frantically ordered, "Drop your knives!"

Dozens of knives clanked to the floor.

"Stop it, stop it!" the wizard shrieked at the wanderer, but that only made him play louder and faster. And the louder and faster he played, the higher and quicker the wizard had to dance. He danced so fast that his many slippers went flying from his feet. Some even went straight up and bounced off the moss on his head.

The wanderer played with all the fear and anger inside him. He was a winter storm barreling down a mountain pass. He was a tidal wave rolling in from the sea.

And all the wizard could do was dance. He stomped on

top of the chest. "You can have all the gold you can carry," moaned the wizard.

With a smile, the wanderer sent the wizard hopping around among the little men. "You can have all my jewels too," the wizard groaned.

Then the wanderer played so hard that the wizard's feet pounded the dirt like hammers—as if he wanted to nail himself right into the mountain. "You can have anything, anything," wailed the wizard.

Keeping a watchful eye on the little men, the wanderer lifted his mouth from the flute long enough to say, "Free the rainbow people."

The wizard smiled for the wink of an eye. "And you'll stop?" he gasped.

"But I'll keep the flute to replace my old one," the wanderer suggested.

"It'll bring you more trouble than joy," the wizard warned.

"Maybe I want it so I can remember you by," the wanderer joked.

"Then play something slow. Something slow and lonely," ordered the wizard.

So the wanderer slowed the music until it was like leaves budding on the tree. Flinging up his arms, the wizard whirled in circles and chanted in low voice. Finally he lowered his arms. "There," the wizard said. "Now you can stop and go see for yourself."

The wanderer looked at all the little men between him and the hole he had made to get into the tree. The dancing wizard motioned them away.

"If you've tried to trick me, I'll be back," the wanderer warned, and then bolted for the hole.

"I kept my bargain." The wizard smiled. "But remember this: Sometimes you lose something in the very act of saving it."

The wanderer expected a horde of little men to chase him as he darted from the tree, but the only thing that followed him was the sound of the wizard's laughter.

Although the path was steep and dangerous, the wanderer ran all the way to the village. At first he thought it was some trick of the moonlight, because the fields seemed full of giant, wriggling worms.

As he got closer, the shapes seemed to grow until he could see that they were dragons. And they weren't just wriggling. They were dancing. Big, powerful creatures with claws sharp as swords; and yet so graceful they almost seemed to float over the fields—like long green streamers embroidered with gold.

But the farmers were nowhere to be seen. They weren't in the fields. They weren't in the village streets either. Finally, he looked inside a hut. Pants and trousers lay on the floor, shredded into rags. Every hut was filled with torn clothing.

He clutched the flute. "The old wizard's tricked me. I'm going to make him dance till his teeth fall out." He was about to storm back up to the mountaintop when he heard a voice like dark velvet.

"No," she said.

He turned around joyfully, but he only saw a golden dragon curled up in a corner.

"I want to thank you," the dragon said.

He leaned forward to stare, and there on her forehead was a gleaming pearl where the circular birthmark had been.

"You didn't tell me," he said.

"You didn't ask."

"How long have you been in his spell?" the wanderer asked.

"For a long time. Too long."

A loud splash came from one end of the valley and a fountain of water rose high over the cliffside. The wanderer saw a dragon spring off the cliffside and then fall like an arrow into the sea. The next moment, there was another loud splash and more foam fountained up.

All over the valley, the dragons were leaving the fields and flowing like leathery streamers toward the sea.

And the wanderer remembered the wizard's words: "Sometimes you lose something in the very act of saving it."

"Good-bye," he said.

"Good-bye." And she followed the other dragons to the cliffside. She was the last to leave; and she looked over her shoulder at him before she leaped high into the air. Then, arching her long, elegant back like a rainbow, she dropped out of sight. Then the water rose behind her like a white peacock tail.

He ran to the edge of the cliffside. But the dragons were already far out to sea, sliding through the glittering reflection of the moon toward the moon itself.

AFTERWORD

The more I worked on these stories, the more I felt that I had simply stumbled upon the same pool of the imagination that others had before me. Furthermore, each storyteller, as part of the initiation into that community, tries to leave a mark upon that pool without changing it—a contradictory task impossible in the world of the physical but quite possible in the world of the imagination.

I have tried to use my own voice to retell the stories while preserving their spirit and spare beauty. However, as with all things that come from the heart rather than the head, I'm also aware that this process was quite arbitrary and subjective.

I am indebted once again to a number of people, including Michael Broschat, Joanne Ryder, Marilyn Sachs, Morris Sachs, and John Kuo Wei Tchen, who are all part

193

of that same community in their own right and who each helped during different stages of this project.

For a general review of Chinese tales and the supernatural, I highly recommend the introduction to Karl S. Y. Kao's *Classical Chinese Tales of the Supernatural and the Fantastic* (Bloomington, Indiana: Indiana University, 1985).

Readers interested in further material might look at the following:

The Golden Mountain, Chinese Tales Told in California, collected and translated by Jon Lee and edited by Paul Radin with notes by Wolfram Eberhard (Taipei, Taiwan: The Orient Cultural Service, 1972).

Folktales of China, edited and translated by Wolfram Eberhard (Chicago: University of Chicago Press, 1965).

Hong Kong Tale-Spinners, compiled and translated by Bertha Hensman (Hong Kong: Chinese University of Hong Kong, 1968).

More Hong Kong Tale-Spinners, compiled and translated by Bertha Hensman (Hong Kong: Chinese University of Hong Kong, 1971).